The Last Act

Kindred Spirits Mysteries

Beth Connor

WOLF GROVE MEDIA, LLC

Contents

CHAPTER ONE

Setting the Stage

Nora Sinclair was out of her element, and she knew it. As she stood in the doorway of the Majestic Theatre, she felt like she'd wandered into a dragon's lair armed with nothing but the clothes on her back. Dance had always been her armor, something she could rely on to win over any audience. But acting? That was a different beast..

She grew up believing she would become a Rockette. There was never any doubt in her mind that she could attain this goal. That is until the paperwork read that she had to be 5'5. So now, here she was, on the brink of a new career, about to step onto the stage with nothing but her wits. She wondered if she was about to take a giant leap—or land flat on her face.

Inside the theater's grand lobby, she thought of her childhood, when she first fell in love with dance. Sports never suited her. She remembered the feeling of the spotlight, the thrill of the music, and the way the world melted away when she was on stage. But acting? Acting made her feel vulnerable, like it put a big target on her back.

She sighed. There had been so many dance auditions where each panel member seemed to look past her, focusing instead on the taller dancers. It wasn't easy being short and curvy while dreaming of a career that demanded a tall, lithe body. Despite training and dedicating her teenage years to ballet, tap, and jazz classes, Nora had remained a steadfast 5 foot 2 and three-quarters. For the Rockettes, those missing inches mattered.

As she reminisced, Nora's thoughts drifted back to how she ended up in Boston. She had grown up in central New Hampshire and back home, people knew her name. When the Radio City Music Hall dream didn't pan out. Her love for the arts led her to Boston, where she studied performing arts and dance at Emerson College. During those years, she fell in love with the city.

After graduating, Nora landed a job teaching dance just outside the city and tried out for as many opportunities as she could find. The *Chicago* audition was on a whim—never in a million years did she think she would get an actual role. She felt hopeful for a part in the dance ensemble, and if she was lucky, one of the "Cell Block Tango" gals. But Roxie Hart? It was an opportunity she couldn't pass up, one that promised to push her harder than she had ever been pushed. But now, as she stood alone, she felt like a sheep in wolf's clothing.

Somehow, Nora Sinclair had landed the lead in a Boston Stage Ensemble's production of *Chicago*. Roxie Hart was a character who owned the stage and charmed everyone around her. And Nora? She was a dancer who had stumbled into a role that required a world of swagger and confidence she wasn't sure she had. Yet here she was, about to tackle the impossible.

The read-through had been manageable, even though her nerves seemed determined to make a spectacle of themselves. The other actors were friendly, offering nods and smiles when she fumbled her lines. But that was just reading words on a page.

Tonight was different. Tonight was the first rehearsal at the theater. Here, she would try to convince everyone—including herself—that she could do this. The prospect was terrifying.

The Majestic Theatre was a relic of another era, with its grand arches, opulent chandeliers, and velvet curtains. Its walls held stories of triumphs and tragedies, laughter, and tears. The air itself seemed to hum with the echoes of past audiences, as if they were waiting to see what stories would unfold.

She took a deep breath and stepped inside, hoping that somewhere within its walls, she'd find the courage to carry her through the night. As Nora moved deeper into the theater, she paused in front of a framed photograph of an actress who had performed there decades ago. The woman's eyes seemed to follow Nora, her knowing smile almost unsettling. A shiver ran down Nora's spine.

She had heard stories about the theater's ghosts, but something about this picture felt different. As she stared at the actress's face, she swore she heard a soft whisper brush past her ear, though the words were too faint to understand. A sudden chill swept over her, sending goosebumps racing up her arms.

Nora leaned in closer, noticing something odd about the photograph. The nameplate was blank, almost as if it had been erased. Who was this woman? Was she one spirit rumored to linger here?

Maybe the ghosts would lend a hand tonight. Or maybe, like everyone else, they'd find her performance as awful as she feared. It didn't matter. She was here now, and there was no turning back. She would channel Roxie Hart—or at least bluff her way through it with the best of them.

The silence was reverent, as if the very walls held their breath. Her footsteps echoed on the polished floor and she looked around, hoping to find another actor to follow. Maybe then she could imitate their rehearsal etiquette. But the lobby was empty, save for the strange shadows cast by the chandeliers.

"Hello?" she called out. Her voice bounced back to her, lingering in the air, reminding her she was very much alone.

The butterflies in her stomach were relentless, doing what felt like a full tap routine. A sudden wave of nausea swept over her. What if this was all some elaborate joke? Maybe she was being punked, and any moment now, someone would leap out from behind a curtain with a camera crew in tow.

Then she heard it—a soft rustling, like fabric brushing against the wall, though no one else was there. The scent of roses lingered in the air. Nora paused, trying to figure out where the noise was coming from. Just as quickly as it began, the sensation vanished, leaving the lobby still and silent once more.

Before she could dwell on it, the door to the house swung open, and the director, Martin Holloway, stepped out.

"Nora," he said, his brow furrowing in mild confusion.

She felt close to tears, her mind racing. "Did I miss rehearsal?"

Martin chuckled, his expression softening. "No, sweetie," he said, patting her on the shoulder. "You're an hour early!"

Nora's face paled to a shade whiter than she already was, and her freckles turned a bright red.

Martin put his arm around her shoulders in a comforting gesture. "It happens to the best of us—and better early than late! Let me show you around, then you can explore a bit before the others get here."

He led Nora through the winding corridors of the Majestic Theatre. The building seemed to have more personality than most people. It wasn't just grand; it was grand with a capital G, and it knew it. The walls were covered in intricate gold leaf patterns, like some sort of ornate wedding cake, and the velvet curtains looked so thick that they could stop a bullet—or at least muffle a sneeze.

"This theater's seen its fair share of drama," Martin said, his voice echoing in the cavernous space. "From its earliest days, it's been a home to actors, musicians, and even a ghost or two."

Nora clutched at her script. The corners crumpled from nervous fidgeting. Martin glanced at the paper and raised an eyebrow, his expression somewhere between amused and fatherly.

"You know," he said, "Roxie's lines are supposed to be memorized by now."

Nora's heart sank like a stone in a pond. Memorized? Nobody told her that! She felt as though she had shown up to the wrong party, wearing a clown costume instead of a ball gown.

"Memorized?" she repeated, her voice squeaked.

Martin chuckled. "Don't worry, Nora. You've got some time before the others arrive. Use it well."

He smiled and continued the tour, showing her the backstage chaos. Then the green room with its ancient couches that had seen more drama than Shakespeare, and the orchestra pit that looked as though it could swallow the entire string section whole.

After Martin's tour, Nora wandered down a narrow corridor lined with posters from past productions. Her fingers brushed against the faded paper. She felt drawn to the past, as if the theater was urging her to uncover its secrets.

The Majestic was a maze of hidden doors and winding staircases, each turn revealing another layer of its character. She felt as if she were inside a giant clock, all gears and pulleys, ticking away as the minutes slipped by.

In the shadows of one hallway, she discovered a small wooden door. She opened it and peered inside, seeing shelves filled with old props and costumes. As she stepped inside, the floorboards creaked underfoot. A sense of history wrapped itself around her. There was something magical about this place.

"This'll do," Nora muttered to herself, brushing off a chair and settling in. The room was dim and smelled like old costumes and varnish, but it was quiet. A perfect place for a bit of last-minute cramming.

She perched on the chair, surrounded by the ghosts of performances past. With only thirty minutes left, she opened her script and read, her voice mingling with the faint noises of the theater, and the building itself leaned in to listen.

Nora was surprised that she had memorized most of her lines and she allowed her attention to drift. Across the room, she noticed a seam in the wall with a curious little indent that almost looked like a handle. She wandered over, deciding to give it a closer inspection.

When she pressed her hand into the indent, the panel popped open with a soft click.

Inside was a small, tarnished tin box, its surface weathered and streaked with age. The faint outline of an engraved pattern, now softened by time, caught the light. She traced a finger over the etching before prying the lid open with a soft creak. A familiar scent. Roses—old, dried, and faint—rose from the box, wrapping around her senses like a distant memory.

Nestled inside was a bundle of letters, yellowed with age and tied together with a faded ribbon that looked like it might disintegrate if she so much as breathed on it wrong. On the top letter, the name "Helen" was scrawled in a bold, masculine hand, the ink dark and smudged in places. Helen. The name tugged at something in the back of her mind, but it was like trying to catch smoke.

Nora's fingers hovered over the letters, itching to untie the ribbon and dive into their contents. Who was this Helen? And who had written these letters to her with such careful strokes? Her imagination wandered—old lovers, tragic endings, secrets never meant to be uncovered. It all felt like the opening chapter to a gothic romance, the kind where she'd soon be fending off cursed paintings or unraveling ghostly mysteries.

She was just about to slide one letter free when her watch buzzed. Nora jumped, startled, out of her reverie. Rehearsal. Of course. She sighed, casting one last glance at the letters. Time had a way of slipping by when you were on the verge of uncovering forgotten stories.

After a minute, she blinked herself back into the present. Careful not to crumple the fragile paper, she tucked the letters back into the tin, fastened the lid, and slipped the whole thing into her backpack.

As she made her way back to the stage, her mind was still half-lost in the past, wondering about this mysterious Z and Helen, and what happened to them. Did they get married? Were they famous actors of the time?

The theater was buzzing with activity now, people milling about, waiting for rehearsal to start. There was a familiar tightening in Nora's chest.. It was like getting ready to leap from a great height, and hoping a net would appear before you hit the ground.

As she waited in the wings, she caught snippets of conversation from the other actors arriving for rehearsal. There was talk of a strange noise backstage, and someone mentioned seeing a shadow flit across the balcony.

"Do you believe in the ghosts?" one whispered to another.

Nora leaned closer, her curiosity piqued.

"Of course," the other replied with a grin. "This place is full of them. But don't worry—they're friendly... mostly."

Nora wobbled. She was relieved to see a few others glancing over their shoulders. Maybe she wasn't the only one who felt the theater's energy humming just beneath the surface.

Martin Holloway was in the wings, deep in discussion with a crew member who was making adjustments to the fly system. Martin's voice was warm and carried across the lobby, mingling with the murmur of other preparations. He had a way of making everyone feel included and capable. This made him not just respected, but cherished among the theater folk.

Nora's gaze drifted to the person Martin was talking to. With an easy familiarity, this individual served as a calm port amid the storm of pre-rehearsal chaos. Their presence eased Nora's frayed nerves. With a gentle smile, a brief, quiet moment of understanding passed between the two of them.

She felt a delightful tug at her heart—like the first page of a story she couldn't wait to read. Their eyes sparkled beneath cropped curls, and a halo seemed to form in the light. Adorned with an array of piercings, they oozed charisma. Something about that smile, simple yet reassuring, helped settle the nerves in Nora's stomach.

"Ready to jump in?" Martin called out, his voice a life-line.

"Yes, I think I am," Nora said, though the words felt hollow in her throat. Her hands trembled as she lowered her backpack in the wing, fingers fumbling over the straps. Each step toward the stage made her knees wobble, a slow, creeping weakness spreading through her legs until it felt like the ground itself might give way beneath her.

Today's rehearsal focused on blocking—no choreography, no music—just the actors finding their place and navigating the bare bones of the performance. It should have been simple. Yet, as Martin called for silence, a tension settled, and Nora's nerves twisted into tighter and tighter knots.

The rehearsal began with Ciera, who played Velma, entering. Ciera was all sharp edges and commanding presence. Her voice filled the theater with an effortless authority that Nora envied.

Then it was her turn. As she stepped forward to embody Roxie Hart confronting Fred, the stage lights blazed down, harsh and unforgiving. She reached for her lines, but instead of words, her mind served up an image of the letters she'd found earlier.

Nora hesitated. "Um..." she stammered, her mind flipping between Roxie and the mysterious letters, and finding neither. The lines were right there, buried under her growing distraction, but she couldn't pull them free. "Line?"

Martin sighed, the tapping of his script against his leg picking up a deliberate, tired rhythm. "Hey, why the hurry? Again, Nora. Focus"

Focus. Right. She blinked, trying to push away the questions gnawing at her brain. Her heart raced as frustration bubbled up—she wasn't just forgetting her lines, she wasn't *present*.

Martin cleared his throat, louder this time.

Nora swallowed hard, casting a quick glance toward the wings. The crew member from earlier caught her eye, offering a slight, encouraging nod. She took a deep breath and her pulse slowed as she exhaled, pushing the thoughts of the letters to the back of her mind. They could wait—*they had to*. She straightened her shoulders and rolled her hands into steady fists at her sides. Roxie needed her attention, not the past.

With a small, determined smile, she stepped forward to attempt her lines again.

"Hey, why the hurry?" Nora began, but her voice wavered, shaky and unconvincing. Her eyes darted to

Fred—portrayed by Lucas, whose confidence on stage felt as natural as breathing.

"Stop," Martin's voice cut through the air, sharp and impatient. "Again, without the nerves, Nora. Please."

She shifted her weight, trying to steady herself, when something caught her eye—a young boy, no older than ten, darting between the seats in the back row, grinning as he weaved in and out of the aisles. Who brings a kid to rehearsal? Wasn't this supposed to be professional? She blinked, thrown off. It seemed odd, but maybe someone on the crew had brought him along.

She opened her mouth to try again, but couldn't shake the distraction. The boy now climbed onto a seat, his slight frame almost bouncing with energy. She furrowed her brow. No one else seemed to notice, which only deepened her unease.

"Nora?" Martin's voice cut through the silence, his frustration barely concealed. "What's going on? You seem a million miles away."

"Sorry, I just—" She hesitated, glancing back toward the boy, who was now perched on the edge of a seat, watching her with that same mischievous grin. "There's a kid running around in the audience."

The room fell still for a beat before a ripple of quiet chuckles spread through the cast. Martin didn't even glance toward the seats, just raised an eyebrow as he sighed. "Kids are not welcome in my rehearsals unless they are cast."

Nora's stomach flipped. She looked again, but the boy was gone. The seats were empty, as if no one had been there at all. A prickle ran up the back of her neck. Had she imagined it?

"I—" She swallowed, her throat dry. "Never mind."

The crew exchanged glances, their smirks not even hidden, and someone muffled a laugh. Nora's face flushed hot, the uneasy feeling gnawing at her insides. Did they think she was losing it?

Martin rubbed his temple, exasperated but resigned. "Let's take it from the top," he muttered, as though he had dealt with this before.

This time, her delivery was smoother. "Hey, why the hurry? Amos ain't gonna be home until midnight." The lines weren't perfect, but they felt more authentic, more hers.

The scene unfolded with Nora's confidence building. By the end of the scene, though far from flawless, Nora found her stride. She wasn't Roxie yet, but she was no longer just Nora. She had moved somewhere in between, finding her footing in a role that seemed as unreachable as the stars.

When the rehearsal concluded, Martin nodded, letting out a long breath. His lips twitched—not quite a grin, but close enough—and his eyes crinkled, suggesting things had gone as he intended.

"Better," he grunted, scribbling notes in his script.

Nora exhaled, the tension in her shoulders easing. *Better* was something, at least. She glanced toward the wings, where the crew member who had been watching earlier gave her a thumbs-up before disappearing behind the curtains.

As the cast began to scatter, Nora lingered, replaying the awkward moment with the boy and the laughter. She was about to head outside when the same crew member approached, offering her a friendly smile.

"Hey, new girl," they said, sticking out a hand. "I'm Alex, by the way. I handle most of the tech stuff around here."

"Nora," she replied, shaking their hand, trying to match their easygoing vibe. There was something about Alex's calm, warm energy that put her at ease, more than she expected.

"You did great up there," Alex said, their smile genuine.

Nora let out a breathy laugh, shifting on her feet. "Not really. It felt like everyone was laughing at me."

Alex shook their head, grinning. "Nah, that wasn't about you. That was because of Ollie."

Nora blinked. "Ollie?" She furrowed her brow, the name not ringing any bells.

Alex glanced around, leaning in, as if letting her in on a secret. "Yeah, the kid you saw in the audience?"

Nora's stomach dropped. "How did you know I saw—" She hesitated, not wanting to sound crazy. "Yeah, I thought I saw a kid running around. No one else seemed to notice, though."

Alex chuckled, their eyes bright with amusement. "That's because most of us are used to him by now. Ollie's one of the theater ghosts."

Nora's heart skipped a beat, and she stared at Alex, waiting for the punchline. "Wait, what? You're telling me that boy was a ghost?"

Alex nodded, their expression casual, as though this was normal. "Yup. Shows up now and then during rehearsals, messes with the new folks. It's kind of his thing."

Nora's mind spun, trying to process this. "So... everyone knew?"

Alex shrugged, a sympathetic smile tugging at their lips. "Pretty much. Martin just ignores it—he's not big on acknowledging the weird stuff. But the rest of us? We're used to Ollie by now. The laughter? That wasn't at you.

It's just part of the ritual when someone new sees him for the first time. Call it a theater hazing tradition, I guess. Welcome to the club."

Nora let out a long breath she didn't realize she was holding. "So I wasn't imagining it?" The knot in her stomach loosened, though she still felt a bit rattled.

"Nope, you really saw him. Don't worry, he's harmless. Likes to play pranks, but he's never caused any trouble. More mischievous than anything."

Nora managed a smile, a strange sense of relief washing over her. "Well, thanks for letting me know. I thought I was losing it."

Alex chuckled. "Nope, you're good. See you tomorrow, Nora."

The streets of Boston were still alive, though the late hour had finally begun to quiet the hum of the city. There was something comforting about it—the way the world slowed, as if it, too, needed a moment to breathe. The streetlights cast a soft, golden glow over the sidewalks, their light guiding her steps as she made her way back to Washington Street.

This was her favorite time of day. The city winding down, the air cool and sharp, and the streets almost hers alone. She let the rhythm of her walk settle into her bones, but her mind, as usual, was elsewhere. Rehearsal. Had she done enough? Could she ever become Roxie Hart, that brash, fearless woman who seemed to inhabit a world so far removed from her own? Doubts curled around her thoughts like stubborn cobwebs she couldn't quite shake off.

But then she remembered the smile—the one that had cut through her nerves like a beam of sunlight. *Alex.* Their quiet confidence in her had meant more than Martin's half-smile ever could. Maybe she wasn't as terrible as she'd feared. Maybe, just maybe, she was good enough.

Her pace slowed as her thoughts drifted to the letters she'd found. The tin box. She hadn't read a word yet, but her fingers itched to pull the letters from her bag. There was a strange excitement bubbling up, like she was teetering on something important—something bigger than herself. The city may have been winding down, but her mind was just starting to stir, full of possibilities.

When she reached her building, the lobby was quiet, save for the soft hum of the elevator that accompanied her ascent. The day had been long, but there was something comforting about the silence here.

Her apartment was a kind of sanctuary. She shared it with two other introverts, roommates who, like her, cherished silence as if it were something rare and precious. They rarely saw each other, and when they did, it was usually in passing—an exchange of nods, maybe a muttered "hey" over a cup of tea. But it worked. There was a rhythm to it all. The quiet companionship of people who understood that sometimes, the best way to live together was to simply not talk too much.

The living room was a delightful mess of mismatched furniture, the kind that seemed to have come together by accident. An armchair slouched in the corner, looking like it had given up on life years ago, while the couch sagged in the middle, as if it had seen one too many people collapse into it after a long day. The shelves were overflowing with books—some precariously stacked, others wedged in at odd angles, as though they'd been read so many times they now demanded to live wherever they pleased. It wasn't elegant by any means, but it had a well-worn charm that made it feel more like home than any magazine-worthy living room ever could.

Her bedroom, though, was the real haven. The walls were a patchwork of posters from past performances, each one a little window into a memory. A small, cluttered desk sat by the window. Dance shoes and leotards lay in a heap on the floor, creating a kind of organized chaos. But it was *her* chaos, the kind that made sense in a way nothing else did. Here, in this little corner of the world, she could breathe. She could dream. It wasn't much, but it was enough.

Nora sat in bed, legs tucked beneath her. The lamp beside her cast a warm light over the mess scattered across the floor. She promised herself she'd clean up tomorrow. Tomorrow was always good for that kind of thing. Right now, she had something far more interesting to deal with.

She reached over to her backpack and pulled out the tarnished tin box. It sat in her lap, heavier than it looked, The metal was cool under her fingers, its engraved design faded with time and handling. There was something old about it, like it had been waiting for her in the theater, gathering dust for decades until she came along.

It felt almost like a treasure chest.

Who didn't love a good mystery? Especially one that involved secret letters tucked away in an old tin box found in a haunted theater. The whole thing was begging for a dramatic reveal—maybe there'd be a tragic love story, or a scandalous affair, or… well, something interesting, anyway. It had to be better than whatever the newest reality TV show on Netflix was.

Nora tilted the box, listening to the soft rustle of paper inside. She hesitated for just a second—what if the letters were just grocery lists?

But that was the thing about mysteries: you didn't know until you looked.

With a little sigh, she popped open the box. The hinges creaked, naturally, like they'd been practicing for this exact dramatic moment. Inside were the bundle of letters. The faint scent of dried roses wafted up, like someone had pressed a bouquet between the pages long ago.

She blinked. That was... poetic.

"Okay," she murmured, reading the name scrawled across the top letter in thick, dark ink. "Let's see what you've got for me."

My Dearest Helen,

I must confess, seeing you on stage today was nothing short of a revelation. You have a presence that commands attention and a voice that lingers long after the last note has faded. It is in those moments that I am reminded of how extraordinary you truly are.

Our rehearsals are the brightest part of my day. Running songs with you, even in the quiet of an empty theater, fills me with a joy that I find hard to express. I hope you will allow me to do so whenever you wish, for there is no greater pleasure than sharing those moments with you.

Please do not doubt your talent or your place on that stage. You are not a fraud, my dear. You possess a gift that is all your own, and I have no doubt that the world will one day come to see it as I do.

Until we meet again in the shadows of the wings, know that my thoughts are with you.

Yours truly, Z.

Nora sat back, the words settling over her like an old, well-worn blanket—familiar, but not in the way she'd expected. It was strange, really, how something written so long ago could feel like it was meant for her. Whoever Helen was, she'd wrestled with the same gnawing self-doubt, the same aching need to belong. Some things, apparently, didn't care about time. Nora folded the letter carefully, her mind buzzing with questions and possibilities as she pulled out the next letter.

Dearest Zeke,

Tonight, as the curtain fell, and the applause roared like a storm, I thought of you, and how your presence fills the empty spaces between the notes. Your faith in me is a light in the dark, a beacon that guides me through the chaos of this world we call the stage.

The world beyond the theater is vast and uncertain, yet with you, I find a place of belonging. Our moments together, though brief, are precious beyond words. It seems the world would prefer our paths not to cross, but in you, I have found a kindred spirit.

Let us face whatever comes with courage and a shared smile, even if they whisper otherwise.

Until our next encounter, know that you are in my thoughts.

Yours affectionately,

Helen

Nora paused, her eyes lingering on the name *Zeke*. She knew their names now. Zeke and Helen. A little thrill ran through her, like she'd just unlocked the first clue in some grand, forgotten puzzle. There was something about a name that made it all feel more real—more tangible. Two people tied together through time, their story tucked away in these hidden letters, waiting for who knows how long.

She frowned, wondering why all the letters had been kept together. It seemed odd—something so private, stashed away in a dusty old theater. Maybe someone had needed them close, a quiet comfort in the shadows. Or maybe the letters had just been patient, waiting decades for the right person to stumble upon them, like some forgotten relic that didn't mind being lost.

With a satisfied nod, Nora refolded the paper, careful not to crease it more than it already was. These letters were a treasure—secret, tucked-away pieces of someone's life, and she could savor them, bit by bit, when the time felt right. She placed the tin box on her desk, feeling an odd sense of contentment. It was there, waiting for her, a quiet little mystery to return to whenever she was ready.

CHAPTER TWO

Cast and Crew

Nora felt like she'd been trampled by a herd of elephants. Every muscle groaned in protest. What made it even stranger was that she hadn't danced at all yesterday—just spent hours obsessively going over the rehearsal in her mind. Apparently, mental gymnastics was just as punishing as the physical kind.

Her body creaked as she got out of bed, each movement reminding her of the awkward tangle of thoughts she'd been stuck in the night before. She'd replayed every flubbed line until Martin's critiques became a symphony of disappointment. Stress, she told herself. It's just stress. It had better be, because she could not afford to get sick right now. Not with rehearsals intensifying.

If she had to be honest, last night's practice had been rough, but it wasn't catastrophic. Still, the little nagging voice in her head was making sure she remembered every mistake in excruciating detail.

She pulled her hair back into a ponytail, her fingers moving on autopilot while her brain went galloping ahead into the day. She hummed, flipping through lesson plans in her mind, trying to convince herself she was organized. The soft morning light trickled through the window, casting gentle, comforting shadows across the walls. This was her space—she should have felt at ease here, but something kept gnawing at the back of her mind, a persistent, uncomfortable feeling.

She glanced around the room, her eyes sweeping over the familiar clutter—scripts piled haphazardly on the desk, dance shoes peeking out from under the bed, and the letter tin sitting on the desk. It was the same space she woke up to each morning. A comfortable chaos that reflected her busy life. Yet today, it felt different. As if the very air around her was charged. She shook off the feeling, telling herself it was just nerves. But the sensation lingered.

Nora opened the tin and lifted a letter, treating it like it might crumble under her touch. As she unfolded the fragile paper, she could almost feel the past pressing against her fingertips. A sudden creak from the floor made her heart leap into her throat. Her eyes shot up, half-expecting to find someone lurking in the shadows. But the room was still, as it had been. She let out a weak laugh, trying to shake off the creeping unease that clung to her.

Still, as she packed the tin back into her bag, she couldn't shake the feeling of being watched. The play of shadows on the walls seemed to deepen, as though the room itself was watching her every move. Was it possible that Helen was there, somehow aware of her intentions to uncover her secrets? She shrugged off the thought, steeling herself for the day ahead. With one last glance around, she grabbed her things and headed out the door.

Today was not a day to think about the letters (at least not until she was back home). She needed to stay grounded and focused. It was the first day of the summer dance session, and she had rehearsal right after classes. While she wasn't able to teach any of this summer's intensives, Linda, the studio owner, had given her all the morning preschool classes.

The little kid's unbridled enthusiasm was contagious, but she was going to miss the challenge of refining technique with older students. Also, the *Chicago* gig paid well. But it would be over in October, and she couldn't afford to give up her teaching job just yet. Balancing both roles was important, even if it meant sacrificing her own training time for the stability she needed.

Fortunately, Linda was incredible. She supported Nora and was rooting for her to succeed. Linda's faith in her was a steadying force, a reminder someone other than her parents believed in her potential. In reality, Linda was nice, but having a big name working for her brought in more business. Nora appreciated Linda saw the mutual benefit and was thankful for her understanding and flexibility.

Nora stepped out of her apartment and was enveloped by the sticky humidity that signaled summer in Boston. The heat clung to her skin, making her hair frizz in the moisture-laden air. She adjusted her backpack and made her way to the nearby station, hoping the train would offer some relief from the morning heat. As she descended the stairs, the air became cooler, offering a brief respite from the oppressive humidity outside. Nora swiped her card at the turnstile and pushed through, joining the crowd of commuters waiting for the next train.

The platform was bustling with the typical morning rush, filled with commuters who seemed to be in a race against time. Nora found herself caught amid it all, trying to focus on her lines for Roxie Hart. Her eyes skimmed the script, but her mind was distracted, flitting between thoughts of her upcoming rehearsal and the letters she'd found in the theater.

The train was running late, and the growing crowd pressed in from all sides. She shifted her weight and glanced down the tunnel, willing the train to arrive. Her attention caught on a familiar figure across the way, a person whose cropped curls and easy smile she recognized—the mysterious crew member from the theater.

Her heart skipped a beat. There was something about their presence that had given her reassurance the previous day. They stood still amidst the bustling crowd, their gaze meeting hers. Nora's eyes caught on a familiar face, and something flickered inside her—almost a smile. Her hand twitched, ready to lift in greeting, but then the train roared into the station. The blast of noise and wind hit her all at once, rattling through her bones. She blinked, disoriented, her thoughts scattering with the rush of air.

As the doors slid open with a mechanical whine, the crowd surged forward, sweeping the mysterious figure into the throng of passengers boarding the train. Nora craned her neck, trying to catch another glimpse of them, but it was as if they had vanished. She stood there, staring at the spot where they had been, feeling a mix of curiosity and disappointment. Questions whirled in her mind. Who were they? Why did their presence feel so significant? Nora boarded the train herself, feeling the pressure of the crowd as she squeezed into a small space by the door.

As she ran her lines in her head, the train approached her stop before she knew it. She glanced at her watch, hoping she wasn't running late, and sighed with relief—it was all in her head. When the train came to a halt, she stepped off and joined the stream of commuters heading toward the exits. The walk from the station to the studio was quick, but the heavy humidity made it feel longer today. As she weaved through the crowd, her mind shifted to the lessons she would teach that morning.

Nora arrived at the dance studio, greeted by the familiar sounds of laughter and chatter. The children's eager faces reminded her why she loved teaching. Their eyes lit up, wide with curiosity and bursting with energy, tiny feet bouncing with every step. As they spun and stumbled, giggling through their wobbly twirls, Nora's heart skipped along with them. Every laugh, every clumsy leap sent a quiet thrill through her, like she was handing down a secret—one of rhythm and grace—wrapped up in their joy.

Even though teaching wasn't her ultimate dream, it was rewarding in its own right. Here, she could nurture their love for dance and see immediate results. She felt a sense of purpose as she helped shape their experiences with dance, knowing she was creating a foundation that might inspire some of them to pursue it further.

After class, Nora moved through the studio, gathering the scattered props and bits of ribbon left behind by the little dancers. The faint scent of sweat and rosin clung to the air, but her smile lingered, her chest still light from the laughter and twirling excitement that had filled the room. The soft patter of tiny feet and the murmur of parents chatting in the hallway faded, leaving the space bathed in a gentle, peaceful quiet. As the last echoes disappeared, Nora felt the floor beneath her cool and steady, the stillness almost soothing. Linda appeared in the doorway, her warm smile as bright as ever. Just seeing her standing there made something in Nora's chest relax—a constant reminder that, here in the studio, she was always surrounded by support and understanding.

"That was a great class," Linda said, stepping inside. "The kids love you."

"Thanks," Nora replied, beaming. "The kids make it easy."

Linda smiled, but her expression shifted, growing more thoughtful as she leaned against the barre. "Actually, I wanted to run something by you. I'm planning a musical theater workshop for November, and I'd love for you to teach it."

Nora's eyes widened, surprise and excitement bubbling up. "Seriously? That sounds incredible! I'd love to."

"I had a feeling you'd be on board," Linda said with a knowing nod. "You've got so much energy and experience to bring, especially with you doing *Chicago* now. Which reminds me—how would you feel about choreographing 'Cell Block Tango' for our competition team?"

Nora's heart leapt, the prospect sending a thrill down her spine. "Are you kidding? I'd *love* to work on that! It would be amazing!" She could feel the choreography already taking shape in her mind, a delicious glimpse into the career she was hungry for.

Linda's grin widened, pleased by her enthusiasm. "I knew you'd be the perfect fit. Once the team's finalized, we can work out the schedule."

"I can't wait," Nora said, her thoughts already racing with ideas and possibilities.

"Great," Linda replied, pushing off the barre. "Let's catch up later this week to go over the details. Friday work for you?"

"Absolutely," Nora agreed. "Thanks, Linda. This really means a lot."

As Linda left, Nora stood there, a surge of excitement coursing through her. The workshop, the choreography—everything she had been hoping for was finally within reach. She felt lighter, more confident, as if the future she'd been working toward was finally starting to take shape. Roxie Hart wasn't the only one going places.

Nora glanced at her watch as she pushed through the doors of the Majestic Theatre—4:30 PM. Just enough time. She hurried down the hall, the click of her shoes echoing against the old walls, and headed straight for the storage room.

Inside, the familiar scent of old costumes and varnish hit her, thick and musty, like a well-worn blanket wrapping around her shoulders. She shut the door behind her with a soft thud, the noise from the theater fading into a dull hum. The rickety chair creaked as she dropped into it, one leg wobbling.

Nora took a slow, steady breath, eyes drifting to the piles of forgotten props and dusty fabric. The theater's chaotic energy couldn't reach her here—not the rush of rehearsals, not the ghostly whispers brushing past her ear. This was her space now, carved out for a few quiet moments before she'd have to step back onto the stage.

A wave of hunger reminded her she hadn't eaten since breakfast. With rehearsal stretching until 9 PM, she needed something to tide her over. She rummaged through her bag and found a squished snack bar, tearing it open. Its crinkled wrapper was a lifeline, promising at least a temporary reprieve from the hunger pangs. She unwrapped the snack bar and took a large bite, the wrapper crinkling in the quiet room. Chocolate and oats, a poor substitute for a proper meal, but better than nothing. The crumbly mess was sticky, and she could feel the sugar coursing through her veins, providing a much-needed energy boost.

Then she started her vocal warm-ups, humming scales and enunciating phrases with her mouth half-full. Halfway through a particularly tricky tongue twister, she realized she must look ridiculous. Bits of the oat bar stuck to her cheek. She wiped the crumbs from her face, laughing at herself. Before she could restart, the temperature in the room dropped. It was as if someone had opened a window to a frigid winter night. Her thoughts went back to the muscle aches she felt that morning, and a sense of dread washed over her. *I will not get sick, I will not get sick,* she repeated as a mantra.

Determined to focus, Nora shifted her posture, standing taller and full of the confidence Roxie Hart would exude. She narrowed her eyes and practiced Roxie's smirk, letting the character's swagger seep into her bones. Just as she began to feel like Roxie, a loud whisper interrupted her concentration. The voice seemed to come from nowhere and everywhere at once, and it was angry. Nora paused, curious, as she strained her ears to listen. The whispering grew louder, yet the words remained elusive. A gust of wind brushed past, leaving the lingering scent of roses in its wake. It was unsettling, as if someone had rushed by her in a hurry—but there was no one there.

A crash sounded from the corner of the room, and her heart lurched. She twisted her head, her mind racing with possibilities. *What was going on?* The whispers intensified, seeming to hiss right by her ear, crescendoing to an almost deafening volume. Whoever or whatever this was, it was angry.

Her fingers dug into the arm of the wobbly chair. The entire room seemed to hum with a strange energy. Whoever—or whatever—was here, it didn't seem happy.

"Who's there?" she squeaked out, her breath tight.

The door creaked open behind her, the sound cutting through the tension. "Hello? Someone in here?"

And just like that, the room stilled. The whispers vanished, leaving only the soft thrum of her pulse in her ears. Nora's grip loosened on the chair. Slowly, she stood, glancing toward the door. The hallway was empty, but as she stepped closer, she caught a glimpse of Alex just rounding the corner.

"Alex?" she called, her voice a little shaky.

They turned, their face lighting up as they spotted her. "Hey, Nora," Alex greeted, walking toward her.

Alex raised an eyebrow. "You alright?"

Nora let out a shaky breath, trying to steady her voice. "Yeah, I—" She swallowed, her words feeling stuck in her throat. "I think so." She glanced around the now quiet room, the sudden warmth of it unsettling after the chill that had run through her moments before. "I just thought... I... heard something."

Alex leaned against the doorframe, a half-grin playing on their lips. "Weird as in 'crash and whispering ghosts' weird?"

Nora's stomach twisted. "You heard that?"

"Didn't have to." Alex stepped inside, brushing past her as if they'd been through this a hundred times. "It's this room. They like to stir things up in here. Ghosts have a sense of humor, I guess."

Nora's pulse quickened, but her fear was giving way to curiosity. "The whispers... are they dangerous?"

Alex shook their head, a spark of amusement in their eyes. "Nah. They're harmless. They like to make noise, throw things around, maybe mess with you if you're new, but they've never hurt anyone. We'd all be in trouble if they were dangerous."

Nora frowned, still eyeing the corners of the room where the crash had come from. "But what was that crash?"

Alex shrugged, like it was no big deal. "Could've been anything. Props shifting, old junk falling over—half the time it's the ghosts just getting bored. This used to be a dressing room back in the early 1900s. Lots of energy trapped here. People who never quite left, you know?"

Nora wasn't sure if she wanted to be relieved or more freaked out. "Has anyone ever tried, I don't know, to get rid of them?"

Alex chuckled. "Oh yeah, a couple of times. Even had one of those ghost-hunter TV shows come in. You know the type—night vision cameras, dramatic voiceovers, the whole deal. They claimed the place was haunted for sure. Pretty sure it got us more ticket sales, though, so Martin didn't mind."

Nora's mouth twitched in a reluctant smile. "So, they're just... here? Doing their thing? Watching us?"

"Pretty much." Alex nodded, crossing their arms. "But they're not dangerous. Well, maybe Ollie's pranks will freak you out, but other than that, it's just noise. Energy. And a lot of history."

Nora let her eyes wander back to the spot where the crash had sounded. The room, now calm, seemed almost normal again, though the thought of ghosts lingering in the shadows still made her uneasy. Yet, at the same time, something about it intrigued her.

"Do they mind if I keep warming up in here?" She asked.

"Mind? Nah. If anything, they'll probably appreciate the company." Alex shot her a wink. "Besides, it's not like they're going anywhere."

Relief washed over Nora. "Thanks, Alex. I think I needed that."

"Anytime," Alex said, giving her a quick, reassuring squeeze on the shoulder. "Now, come on. Martin's getting things moving. You ready?"

Nora glanced around the room. "Yeah," she said, her voice steadier now. "I think I am."

CHAPTER THREE

Overture

Last night's rehearsal had been better than the first, but that wasn't saying much. Nora still felt like the greenest actor on the stage, sticking out like a sore thumb—or maybe a sore everything. The number of times Martin had swapped her out for Lexi was... alarming, to say the least. Every time he called Lexi forward, Nora felt her stomach twist into a tighter knot. But what could she do? She just had to keep pushing through.

Lexi, of course, made it all look so easy. She glided across the stage with the confidence that made Nora feel like she was wearing someone else's shoes—too big. Lexi had been at this for years, and Nora? Well, she was still learning how to keep her knees from locking up when the lights hit her.

But she wasn't about to give up. Not now. She'd come in early today, hoping to steal some quiet practice time before everyone else showed up. Maybe, if she was lucky, she could catch Martin and talk through her progress, prove she was serious about the role. That knot in her stomach had settled into a hard, determined lump. She'd prove herself.

The room seemed to welcome her today. No chilly air, just the faint, comforting smell of roses. As she began some vocal warm-ups, her eyes kept wandering to her backpack. She took the tin everywhere with her now, but she had not rewarded herself with the chance to read another letter. Perhaps today was the day. Perhaps Zeke's letters would remind her that perseverance was key and that, like Helen, she needed to trust in her abilities.

She finished her warm-ups, feeling her voice grow stronger and more assured with each note. The tin continued to beckon to her, promising secrets and encouragement from those who had faced their own trials.

Nora couldn't help herself, so she reached for the tin and pried it open. She unfolded the next letter, half-expecting it to crumble in her hands. Helen's words flowed across the page, and Nora hoped something she read might lend her the same grit that had carried Helen through her struggles. Maybe it could give her a nudge to believe in her own. Heaven knew she could use it today.

My Dearest Zeke,

I scarcely know where to begin, for my heart is so full after our last meeting. How fortunate was the day when our paths first crossed at the Majestic Theatre! Your music, so vibrant and true, has been a balm to my soul and has filled my days with a joy I had long thought lost. In your presence, the world seems to shine with a new light, one that has given me hope in the darkest of times.

We stand, my dear Zeke, against the tides of convention and expectation. Society, with its relentless gaze, seeks to confine us within its rigid walls, yet my heart remains steadfast and unwavering in its affection for you. There are whispers of disapproval, eyes that linger too long, but know that my love is resolute and boundless, transcending the barriers that seek to divide us.

I must confess my concerns about Catherine, my understudy. She watches me with eyes sharp as daggers, her ambition palpable in every glance. She covets the role I hold, and there are moments when I ponder whether it would be wise to relinquish it to her. Yet, my passion for the stage and my belief in our shared dream urges me to persevere. Still, her presence is a shadow upon my thoughts.

Let us not surrender to fear, for in you I have found a kindred spirit, a love that defies all conventions. Together, we shall face whatever trials may come, hand in hand.

Yours devotedly,

Helen

Nora refolded the letter and tucked it back into the tin. The actress's worries about Catherine felt familiar, like they had jumped through time and landed right in Nora's lap. She could feel Catherine's sharp stares, the same way she sometimes caught Lexi eyeing her during rehearsals. It wasn't overt, but there was no mistaking the quiet ambition behind Lexi's glances, and honestly, it unsettled Nora more than she cared to admit.

But Helen had dealt with this same tension over a hundred years ago, and she hadn't let it stop her. That thought settled Nora's nerves a bit. If Helen could push through understudy drama and stay in the spotlight, then Nora could do the same with Lexi.

Challenges weren't meant to be roadblocks, but large boulders on a path you had to clamber over. Helen seemed to say as much, and though Nora despised scrambling over obstacles, the thought of tackling them was far more appealing than retreating. After all, mountains could be climbed, provided you had sturdy shoes and were willing to get a little dirty.

Nora checked her watch to see how much time she had left before rehearsal. To her relief, she had plenty. Perfect. She could spend a few more minutes with her newfound friends from the past. She smiled to herself and unfolded the letter, eager to see what wisdom it might contain.

My Dearest Helen,

Your words are a treasure that I hold close to my heart. Your courage and grace inspire me daily, and I am in awe of the strength you possess. Never, my beloved, should you entertain the notion of relinquishing your role to Catherine, for it is you who brings life to the stage. Fear must never be given the power to dictate your path.

In my dreams, I envision a world where our love is not shadowed by prejudice and judgment. I believe fervently that music and love possess the power to transcend these barriers, uniting us in a future of harmony and peace.

Though the world outside may be harsh, let us cling to our dreams. Our bond, forged in the fires of adversity, is unbreakable. Together, we shall find our place where we are free to be as we truly are.

With all my love and admiration,
Zeke

Zeke's words were filled with love and longing, but there was something else woven into the lines—an undercurrent of fear and defiance. He spoke of prejudice and judgment as if they were tangible enemies to be battled every day.

Sitting there in the dim light, Nora wondered what it must have been like for them. Why did they face so much disapproval? What was it about their relationship that drew such ire? Was it merely the era they lived in, or something more insidious?

She frowned, tapping the tin with her fingers. Relationships back then must have been so different. The theater had been built in 1903, so these letters had to be written after that. Had Helen been expected to marry someone her family chose for her? Did they still do that sort of thing at the turn of the century? Nora had read enough Victorian novels to know that arranged marriages were common, but this was America, not some European court. Surely people could choose for themselves by then... right?

Zeke and Helen had a bond that defied the norms of their time. It was a reminder of how many things had changed and yet, in some ways, stayed the same.

She tried to imagine what it would be like to have her life planned out for her, her choices constrained by expectations and propriety. It made her a little queasy to think about. Nora had never been one to follow rules just for the sake of it, and the thought of being forced into a mold by society made her itch to run the other way.

Setting the tin aside, she resolved to learn more about the era they lived in and what might have stood in their way. Perhaps there were answers buried in the theater's dusty archives—or maybe even within the letters themselves. Whatever the case, she felt an urge to uncover the truth about Zeke and Helen, driven by a desire to honor their courage and perhaps learn from their struggle.

Her curiosity burned, and she couldn't help herself. The questions demanded answers, and the next letter was waiting for her. Anticipation was electric, like the moment just before stepping onto the stage. What secrets might this one reveal? As she unfolded the paper, she devoured each word, hoping to learn more about the lives and loves of these two kindred spirits.

My Dearest Zeke,

I write to you with a heavy heart, for there are matters that weigh upon my soul. Edward Pritchard's attentions grow ever more intrusive and unsettling. His presence at the theater is like a dark cloud, casting shadows over the joy I find in our craft. He has made his interest in me abundantly clear, yet he remains unaware of the true object of my affections. Were he to discover the truth, I fear the consequences would be dire.

The world seems to close in around us, and yet my thoughts remain fixed on a future where we might be free of these chains. Once the curtain falls on our performance, my dearest wish is to leave this life behind and find a haven where we can live without fear. But where might such a sanctuary exist? My heart longs to flee with you, yet I tremble at the uncertainty of our path.

Still, I draw strength from your presence, and I am emboldened by the love that binds us. Together, we shall find our way through this darkness.

With all my love and hope,

Helen

Nora sat back. A new player had entered the scene—Edward Pritchard. The name sent a shiver down her spine and Helen's descriptions of him conveyed his presence was more than just bothersome; it was downright ominous.

Pritchard. Where had she heard that name before? Nora chewed her lip, racking her brain. Of course! The Pritchard family name was practically etched into the very walls of the theater. They were the sort of benefactors who funded art and culture, probably to make up for a past of unsettling dalliances in dark corners.

This was an opportunity to learn more about Helen and Zeke. The Pritchard family was prominent. There had to be clues scattered throughout the archives. Old newspapers, dusty playbills, and perhaps even a gossip column or two might offer glimpses into the time and place Zeke and Helen were from. She was like a detective!

Nora refolded the letter, determination settling into her bones. Uncovering the story of Helen and Zeke had become more than a passing fancy. It had become a mission!

Her fingers itched to read just one more letter. After all, she was on a roll, and there was no time like the present. Nora smiled to herself and reached for the next letter, eager to dive back into the lives of these long-gone lovers.

My Dearest Helen,

The winds of change are upon us, and I have made arrangements that I hope will lead us to a brighter future. My cousin in the Barbary Coast has written to me of a place where cultures mingle freely, and the constraints of society hold less sway. It is there, in the vibrant heart of San Francisco, that I believe we can begin anew.

The journey will not be without its challenges, but I am resolute in my desire to protect you from Edward and his insidious threats. He has begun to encroach upon my life as well, but I stand firm in my resolve to shield you from harm. His influence may be vast, but our love is greater still.

I shall secure passage for us both, and when the time is right, we shall depart this place and seek our refuge. Know that I am with you always, in spirit and in heart, and that no force on this earth shall keep us apart.

With all my love and determination,

Zeke

The mention of the Barbary Coast intrigued her. It sounded like a place full of possibilities, where people of all kinds might gather without the usual fuss and bother.

Then it struck her, the realization that had been hovering just out of reach: Zeke might have been black. The way he wrote about a place where "cultures mingle freely" and the mention of "constraints of society" suggested that their love crossed not just social boundaries but racial ones, too.

It was obvious why they faced such fierce disapproval and why Edward's threats felt so ominous. In those days, a relationship like theirs wasn't just frowned upon; it was dangerous. Their love was a bold act in a time when the world was not accepting of such unions.

Nora leaned back, her chest aching. This wasn't just a love story—it was a quiet rebellion. The kind that takes a lot more courage than anyone ever gives it credit for. She tried to picture what it must have been like, living in a world where society seemed determined to trip you up at every step. Exhausting, probably. Maddening, definitely. It made her feel oddly grateful for how much had changed, but also annoyed, because somehow, it wasn't enough. The world had inched forward, sure, but not nearly as far as it liked to pretend.

The room seemed to hold its breath, the air thick with silence, like even the walls had paused to listen. Nora took a sharp breath—somewhere between a sigh and a laugh, though neither felt quite right. Zeke and Helen's story stuck to her like a stubborn melody, bittersweet and impossible to shake. What had happened to them? Had they escaped, or had their plans fallen apart right here, in the very dust she was kicking up now? She pictured the theater—its creaky floors and lurking shadows—watching it all unfold with cold indifference, just like it always had.

Just then, Alex's head appeared in the doorway. "Hey, Nora, Martin's looking for you."

Nora blinked, shaking off the fog of the past. "Oh. Thanks, Alex," she replied, folding the letter with care and tucking it back into the tin.

She stood up, brushing imaginary dust off her pants, and took a moment to gather herself. The echoes of Zeke and Helen's story were in the forefront of her mind, a reminder that courage could be found in the unlikeliest of places—even in old letters hidden away in a dusty corner. Nora paused for a moment, then pushed the stage door open. The light spilled out into the hallway, beckoning her forward. Whatever Martin had to say, she was ready to hear it.

Nora found Martin leaning against the backstage wall, flipping through a script. She took a moment to steady herself before approaching him.

"Hey, Martin, you wanted to talk?" she asked, trying to keep her voice casual even though her nerves felt like a troupe of hyperactive squirrels.

Martin looked up from his script as Nora approached, his sharp eyes softened. He tucked the pencil behind his ear and nodded for her to sit beside him. "Nora," he started, his tone gentle but direct. "I've been watching your rehearsals, and I think we should talk about where things are at."

Nora's stomach flipped, her nerves jangling like a bad cymbal crash. She sat down, gripping the chair as if it might steady her. "I know I'm still pretty green," she said, forcing her voice to sound steadier than she felt. "But I'm working on it."

Martin leaned back, crossing his arms as his gaze lingered on her, not judging, but searching. "You've got a lot of raw energy, and that's great. You have something real in there. But sometimes it's like you're holding back. You hesitate, and I can see it."

She dropped her eyes, a sigh slipping out as her shoulders sagged under the truth. He wasn't being harsh, and that was the hardest part. He was right. "Why did you pick me for this role?" The question came out quieter than she intended, like it had been hiding at the back of her mind, waiting for the right moment to escape.

Martin's chuckle was soft, almost affectionate, and it echoed through the empty theater. "Because you remind me of Roxie. She's trying to make it in a world that doesn't feel like hers, through sheer grit and determination. She's crafty, ambitious—hell, maybe a little ruthless when she needs to be. But underneath all that, she's just trying to survive, to find her place. I see pieces of that in you."

Nora blinked, her breath catching in her throat. His words hit deeper than she'd expected, unearthing a part of herself she wasn't sure she was ready to look at. "I guess... yeah, there's some of that in me," she admitted, her voice thick with something she didn't understand.

Martin leaned forward, his gaze softening as he looked her in the eye. "You just need to commit, Nora. Let Roxie take over—no half measures. Dive in, give her everything you've got, or the audience will know you're holding back. And you don't want them to see that, right?"

She swallowed hard, the truth of it settling into her like a stubborn cat finding the coziest spot in her soul. "I will," she promised, the words almost a whisper. "I'll give her everything."

His hand found her shoulder, firm but kind. "I believe you will. Now go out there and show them the Roxie you've got inside. Make them remember."

As she stood to leave, Nora felt something shift between them—a quiet understanding, like Martin wasn't just her director, but someone who saw her, really saw her. And that, maybe more than anything, was what gave her the strength to believe in herself.

CHAPTER FOUR

Act 1

On Saturday morning, Nora awoke to the low rumble of thunder, the sound reverberating through the thick, humid air. The heat was oppressive, even this early, clinging to her skin like a damp second layer. Outside, the clouds hung low and heavy. They were the kind that promised a storm but seemed in no hurry to deliver it. It was the weather that made the city feel restless, as if it, too, was waiting for something to break.

Rehearsals had improved since her talk with Martin. Something had shifted. His belief in her had sparked something she hadn't even realized she was missing. But, if she was honest, there was something else at play. Something that gnawed at her—a strange obsession she couldn't shake.

Helen and Zeke. Characters out of a love story, only this wasn't fiction. Their letters had sunk their claws into her. Zeke's words were full of encouragement. If he could believe in Helen, maybe she could believe in herself, too. At least on stage, when she lost herself in Roxie's brash confidence. It felt good—like slipping on someone else's skin and leaving her own doubts behind.

Off stage, the letters wouldn't leave her mind. Zeke and Helen lingered, their story haunting her thoughts. Secret glances, whispered promises, the way they clung to each other in a world bent on tearing them apart—she imagined it all. The decision to dig deeper had already been made. Their story deserved more than to be forgotten.

Last night, she'd stayed up too late reading, her only company the flicker of a single lamp. She swore she could smell roses coming off the old pages, even though she knew that was just her brain being overdramatic. The letters hadn't given her all the answers she wanted, but they made one thing clear: she needed to dig deeper.

The last few letters had been a whirlwind. Zeke and Helen plotting to escape Boston, clinging to desperate hope. But just when she thought she was getting somewhere, the tone of their writing shifted, their words twisting into riddles. Caution crept in, like they were speaking in code.

As she lay there now, listening to the storm gathering strength, she felt that same pull. The library was waiting for her. Today, she would dig deeper. She would find out who they were, these two lovers who had reached across time to touch her life.

With a sigh, Nora pushed herself out of bed, the wooden floor cool against her bare feet. She threw some clothes on, the humid air making them stick to her skin. Outside, the thunder grumbled again, louder this time, as if the sky was finally ready to let loose. She grabbed her bag, tucking the tin inside as if they were a talisman, and headed out into the morning, determined to beat the rain.

It was only a fifteen-minute walk to the library, and she almost made it. But just as she was passing through Copley Square, the skies opened with a sudden, deafening roar, releasing a deluge that soaked her within seconds. The muggy air turned cool and sharp as the rain pelted down.

With a gasp, Nora made a mad dash for Trinity Church, her shoes splashing through the puddles as she raced across the slick pavement. The towering church loomed ahead, its dark stone and red sandstone contrasting with the stormy sky. She reached the sanctuary, ducking beneath the arches.

Nora's heart pounded, the sound drowned out by the hammering of the rain against the cobblestones. In a panic, she yanked her bag open and pulled out the tin, her fingers trembling as she fumbled with the latch. She held her breath, praying the seal had held, that the sudden onslaught had n't ruined the precious letters inside.

With an exhale of relief, she found the tin dry and the letters safe. Nora sagged against the cool stone behind her, letting the tension drain from her shoulders as the rain continued to pour just inches away.

She stayed huddled under the archway; the rain drumming on the stone steps in front of her, creating a misty spray that drifted toward her like a fine veil. But the storm raged on, the sky a churning mass of dark clouds that crackled with the occasional flash of lightning, followed by a growling rumble of thunder. The square, usually bustling with people, was deserted, transformed into a shimmering, rain-soaked landscape.

After what felt like an eternity, The rain eased and the downpour softening to a steady patter. The sky was still overcast, but the worst of it had passed. Nora tucked the tin back into her bag and stepped out into the square.

The library wasn't far, and once inside, the imposing marble lions flanking the entrance seeming to watch her approach with a stern gaze. She hurried up the wide steps, grateful to be out of the rain, and made her way through the maze of rooms and corridors.

Nora's pulse quickened as she made her way to one of the library's most tucked-away treasures—the microfiche room. There was something about the room that held a magic no one else seemed to understand, like an old secret only she was in on. She knew it was an odd hobby—most people would have clicked through a website and called it a day—but for her, this was where the past felt most alive.

As a kid, she'd spent entire afternoons at the Concord Public Library, sitting in the same hunched-over posture, her fingers sliding across the yellowed film strips. Births, deaths, lives boiled down to a few stark words—so impersonal, and yet so intimate. It was like wandering through a graveyard made of stories, the beginning and end of someone's world crammed into a few lines of faded newsprint. She wasn't sure what had drawn her to it back then, but even now, the thrill hadn't worn off.

The familiar dim lighting of the microfiche room greeted her, as did the musty, metallic smell of old film. The walls were lined with drawers, each containing years of forgotten stories waiting to be rediscovered. She found an empty station and slid into the chair, her fingers tracing the edges of the machine before powering it on. The soft whir and click brought a smile to her lips, a comforting sound from a time when she could lose herself in the quiet, slow work of digging through the past.

Sure, the records were digitized now—just a few clicks away—but that was too easy. It felt distant, detached. Here, with the flicker of film and the hum of the machine, she could *feel* the history between her fingers. She selected a reel of playbills from the Majestic Theatre; the film crinkling as she loaded it into the machine. There was a ritual to it—the click of the reel locking into place, the faint glow of the screen, the delicate art of scrolling at just the right speed so you missed nothing.

The first images flickered to life on the screen, a flicker of black-and-white that felt more alive than anything on the internet ever could. It wasn't just research. It was like opening a window into another world, one that whispered secrets only she could hear.

She turned the dial, images flashing across the screen in grainy black and white. It wasn't long before a name leapt out at her—Helen O'Donnell. Her pulse quickened as she adjusted the focus, centering the playbill on the screen. *The Storks*, a musical comedy, had graced the Majestic in the summer of 1905.

As she leaned in closer, a faint whiff of roses drifted by, startling her. The scent was so out of place, yet so familiar, that it made her pause. This had to be it—the connection she had been searching for.

She scrutinized the program, her eyes scanning each line for any sign of Zeke. But there was nothing. If Zeke had been a black musician, would he have even been credited? The thought of his name lost to history filled her with a deep sadness. Yet, despite the absence of his name, something inside her whispered that this was the right trail.

Knowing the play had run in the summer of 1905, she turned to the Boston Globe headlines for June, July, and August of that year. She scrolled through the dates, hope flickering alongside a growing frustration as each page revealed nothing of note.

Then, just as she was about to give up, a headline blazed across the screen: "Local Actress Murdered!" Nora's breath caught in her throat. Hands trembling, she brought the article into focus.

Local Actress Found Murdered in Her Dressing Room

Boston, August 18, 1905—The theater community was rocked yesterday by the tragic news of the untimely death of Miss Helen O'Donnell, a beloved actress known for her recent performances at the Majestic Theatre. Miss O'Donnell, just 24 years of age, was discovered in her dressing room late Monday evening following a performance of *The Storks*, a popular musical comedy in which she played a leading role.

Authorities were called to the scene after Miss O'Donnell failed to emerge from her curtain call. Upon investigation, they found the young actress lifeless, the apparent victim of foul play. Early reports suggest that Miss O'Donnell had been strangled, though the exact details are still under investigation.

In a shocking turn of events, Mr. Ezekial Turner, a musician employed at the Majestic Theatre, was arrested after Miss O'Donnell's body was discovered. Mr. Turner had been working with the theater's orchestra for several months and was reportedly seen leaving the vicinity of Miss O'Donnell's dressing room just moments before her death.

Witnesses claim to have overheard exchanges between the two in the days leading up to the tragedy, leading to speculation that a personal dispute may have been the motive. Police have stated that evidence found at the scene, including a vial of poison, points to Mr. Turner's involvement in the crime.

The trial, which concluded with remarkable swiftness, saw Mr. Turner convicted of murder in the first degree.

Despite his protestations of innocence, the jury returned a guilty verdict after just three hours of deliberation. The conviction has sparked controversy, with some questioning the fairness of the proceedings.

Miss O'Donnell's untimely death has left a void in Boston's artistic circles, where she was known for her talent and charm both on and off the stage. Friends and colleagues describe her as a rising star, destined for greatness in the world of theater. Her loss will be deeply felt by all who knew her.

Ezekial Turner now faces the harshest penalty under the law for his crimes. Meanwhile, the city mourns the loss of a promising young talent, whose life was tragically cut short by a crime that has left many unanswered questions.

Oh, Zeke—it can't be.

Nora stared at the article, her eyes moving over the words again and again as if they might somehow change on the third or fourth reading. *Helen O'Donnell murdered in her dressing room. Ezekial Turner, convicted.* She rubbed her temples, trying to force it all into some kind of shape that made sense.

But it didn't.

The Zeke from the letters, the one who had written to Helen with such tenderness, who had believed in her so fiercely—how could that Zeke have done this? How could he have killed the woman he adored? The two pieces didn't fit together, no matter how hard she pushed.

Nora's breath hitched, and she glanced up, half-expecting to find the ghosts of Helen and Zeke staring back at her from the dim corners of the library. But the room was just as it had been, empty except for the low hum of the microfiche machine.

The kind, gentle man from the letters—*her* Zeke—couldn't be the same man who was convicted of murder. She knew it. But the more she tried to hold on to that certainty, the more it slipped away, like trying to grip water. What if she was wrong? What if the letters had just been Zeke's way of covering up guilt, or worse—manipulating Helen? She shook her head. No. That didn't feel right either.

Her hands clenched into fists. It *wasn't* right.

She took a shaky breath. It didn't matter what the article said. This was the same man who had called Helen a kindred spirit, who had written about her voice lighting up his day. *There had to be more to the story.* She could feel it in her gut, like the strange brief twinge you get when you know you've left something behind, but can't quite remember what it is.

But how was she supposed to prove the innocence of a man who had been dead for over a century? She let out a bitter laugh. "Yeah, Nora, just a casual afternoon hobby—proving a ghost didn't commit murder."

Still, she couldn't let it go. He couldn't have done it, and if no one else was going to clear his name, then maybe it had to be her.

But where the hell do you start with something like that?

She sat back in her chair, the cool metal biting into her back as she stared at the microfiche machine. It wasn't like she could just stroll into the local courthouse and request a century-old trial transcript. Did they even keep records that far back? What if there was nothing to find?

Her eyes narrowed. Well, there had to be *something*.

At the very least, she had a name. Ezekial Turner. There had to be something on him in the records, some thread she could pull. She tucked the microfilm away, her movements sharper now, more purposeful. She had no clue where this path might lead, but she knew one thing for sure: she couldn't stop now.

Gathering her things, she headed for the main desk, the idea of the genealogy department ticking at the back of her mind. She'd always heard they were good at finding old records and tracking down family histories. It was a long shot, but maybe it was the first step toward untangling this mess.

As she approached the librarian, her mind buzzed with a nervous energy. Zeke's face, or at least the version she'd built from his letters, flashed in her head. She wasn't sure if she was about to make the biggest mistake of her life, chasing ghosts and riddles, or if she was on the verge of something huge. Either way, she was committed now.

The librarian looked up from behind the desk, his round glasses slipping down his nose. He smiled, a little too eagerly. Probably bored out of his mind, Nora thought. Well, at least one of them was having a good day.

"Hi," Nora began with a tentative smile. "I was wondering where I could find the genealogy department? And what do I need to access the information there?"

The librarian's eyes lit up with interest. "Genealogy, huh? That's always exciting. You're in luck—our specialist is available today. Let me show you where it is." He stood up with enthusiasm, motioning for her to follow him. "Do you have a particular ancestor or family line you're researching?"

"Not exactly," Nora replied, her voice steady despite the uncertainty gnawing at her. "I'm trying to find more information about a man named Ezekial Turner. He lived in Boston around 1905."

"Ah, historical research! Even better." The librarian's excitement was contagious. "We have plenty of resources for that. Census records, city directories, old newspaper archives—those can all be goldmines for this kind of thing. And if there's anything specific you're after, the specialist can help guide your search."

As they walked, the librarian explained that the genealogy department was one of the library's hidden gems, filled with tools for tracing family histories and uncovering long-forgotten stories. Maybe this was the help she needed.

They reached a door marked "Genealogy and Local History," and the librarian pushed it open, revealing a room lined with shelves full of thick volumes and computers dedicated to genealogical research. The air smelled of the promise of discovery.

"Here we are," the librarian said, gesturing around the room. "I'll introduce you to the specialist—she's brilliant with historical mysteries. If there's something to find about Ezekial Turner, she'll help you uncover it."

Behind the oak desk sat a woman with steel-gray hair pulled back into an immaculate bun, her sharp eyes focused on the computer screen in front of her like she was on the verge of uncovering some great mystery. The click of keys stopped as she looked up, a quick, assessing glance that made Nora feel like she was the mystery.

"Dr. Harris, we've got someone here who could use your expertise," the librarian said, a note of excitement in his voice, like he was handing over a treasure map. "I'll leave you in good hands."

The woman stood, offering her hand with a smile that was both kind and no-nonsense. "I'm Dr. Lydia Harris, but please, call me Lydia."

"Nora," she replied, shaking the woman's hand, feeling a little awkward under that sharp gaze. "Nora Sinclair. I'm trying to find information about a man named Ezekial Turner. He lived in Boston around 1905, and..." She hesitated, unsure how to condense the storm of emotions into something that wouldn't make her sound like she was chasing ghosts. "Well, I think he was involved in a tragic event. I've found some things, but I need to dig deeper. Especially if there's anything about his family."

Lydia's eyes sharpened, not with suspicion but with the same curiosity that had led Nora here. That hungry need to know, to find the thread and pull until the entire story unraveled. "Well, that sounds interesting," she said, sitting back down with a little hum of ap-

proval. "Let's start with court records. If he was convicted of anything, we should be able to track him down."

Nora watched as Lydia's fingers flew across the keyboard, navigating the tangled web of history with the ease
of someone who had spent years learning to speak its language. The clack of keys filled the room as the seconds
stretched, heavy with anticipation.

Lydia's eyes flicked back to the screen. "Ah. Here we
go." Her voice softened, but it had a finality. "Ezekial
Turner. Convicted of murder in 1905. Executed later that
year—November 3rd."

The words hit Nora like cold water, and for a moment,
she forgot how to breathe. She had known, of course. The
article had practically screamed it. But seeing it there in the
dry language of the records—just a date and a crime, as if
that was all a person was—made it feel more real. Too real.

"Executed," she repeated, the word tasting bitter on her
tongue. Poor Zeke.

Lydia glanced at her, and her expression softened,
becoming something almost motherly. "Let's not stop
here. Sometimes the official story isn't the real one." She
turned back to the screen. "Let's see if we can trace his
family line. Sometimes they hold pieces of the puzzle the
records can't show us."

Nora nodded, feeling the tightness in her chest ease a little. The hope, however faint, flickered back to life.

After a few more taps on the keyboard, Lydia's mouth curved into a small smile. "Ah, here's something. It looks like Ezekial had a brother. And his direct descendant—a man named Calvin Turner—is still in Boston. In fact, it looks like he's recently done one of those genealogy DNA tests and made the results public."

Nora's pulse picked up. "Calvin Turner? Do you have an address?"

Lydia scribbled the details onto a slip of paper and handed it to her. "Here you go. If he's interested enough to make his history public, he's probably got more than the bare facts. Families like his have stories, traditions. The kind of things that get passed down but never make it into the official records. He might have exactly what you need."

Nora stared at the paper in her hand, her fingers curling around it like it was a lifeline. "Thank you, Lydia. This is more than I could have hoped for."

Lydia smiled, the sharpness in her eyes now replaced with something kinder. "You're welcome, Nora. I hope it helps. And if you find anything particularly interesting—well, I'd love to hear about it." She winked, the curiosity still bright in her gaze.

Nora nodded, her mind already racing ahead to Calvin Turner, to Zeke, to the pieces of the past she hadn't even uncovered yet. There was a weight to it all, but for the first time, it felt like she might be able to carry it.

The rain outside had slowed to a drizzle, but the sky still threatened more. Walking would have been nice, giving her time to gather her thoughts, but the risk of getting drenched again wasn't worth it. She tucked the paper safely into her pocket and made her way to the nearest T station.

The train ride felt like it took forever. As they emerged from the tunnel, the view opened up to quieter neighborhoods, where the chaos of downtown dissipated. Forest Hills was a neighborhood with its own rhythm, slower and steadier, with streets lined by old trees whose branches hung low.

The houses here were sturdy and unpretentious, their porches adorned with flower pots and wind chimes that tinkled in the breeze. Nora's tension eased as she walked, the calmness of the place seeping into her bones.

She followed the winding streets, her heart picking up speed with each step as she approached the address Lydia had given her. The house was small and neat, with a pale green exterior and a front yard dotted with bright, cheerful marigolds. The windows were framed with dark shutters, and a weathered welcome mat lay in front of the door.

Nora hesitated for a moment at the foot of the porch steps. This was her chance to learn more about Zeke, and she did not know what she would find—or if Calvin Turner would even be willing to talk. She shook off her nerves, climbed the steps, and knocked on the door.

For a long moment, nothing happened. The neighborhood was so quiet that she could hear the rustle of leaves and the distant chirp of a bird. Nora's heart sank thinking she'd come all this way for nothing. But then, from inside, she heard a thud followed by quick, heavy footsteps. Someone was coming.

The door swung open, and Nora stared straight into the eyes of Alex, the stage manager from the Majestic Theatre.

CHAPTER FIVE

A Chorus Line

"Hi," Nora squeaked.

Alex flashed a wide smile, the kind that could melt ice in the dead of winter. "Well, look at this! Is this your new method for rehearsals—popping up at people's houses unannounced?"

Nora's cheeks burned a bright crimson, and she stumbled over her words. "No! I—um—"

"Relax," Alex said, their voice like honey. "I'm just teasing. No harm done. Besides, you clearly didn't expect to find me here, did you?"

"No..." Nora giggled, the sound a bit too breathy as if she were trying to laugh off the butterflies in her stomach. She steeled herself. "I'm actually looking for a Calvin Turner."

"Ah," Alex replied, their smile shifting. "That would be my grandfather. You've come to the right place. Let me grab him for you. Please, come on in."

They swung the door open wider, revealing a small living room. Every available surface was crammed with books, magazines, and what looked like half-finished craft projects. A large, worn sofa sagged in the middle, covered in an eclectic assortment of crocheted blankets that seemed to clash with each other in a way that somehow worked.

Alex wove through the chaos of the living room with a casual grace that spoke of long practice—probably the kind that comes from growing up around a grandparent with a love for both hoarding and storytelling. Nora, stuck in the doorway, felt a bit like she'd wandered into a colorful storm. Somewhere down the hall, a low conversation carried over, punctuated by a chuckle that was amused or surprised, hard to tell. She caught snatches—something about "unexpected visitors" and "rehearsals"—before Alex reappeared, their grandfather trailing behind with a look that was equal parts curiosity and suspicion.

Calvin Turner was small, but he carried himself with the energy of someone twice his size. The family resemblance to Alex was obvious—those sharp cheekbones and the kind of bright, sharp eyes that missed nothing.

"Well, well," Calvin said, his voice a smooth drawl that sounded an awful lot like Alex's, only with more history behind it. He gave Nora a long once-over, eyes narrowing in a way that was both friendly and suspicious, like he was trying to figure out if she was going to pull a rabbit out of her hat. "You related to us? 'Cause I can't say folks usually show up claiming to be interested in the Turner family without some blood ties. Feels a little... odd, doesn't it?"

Nora's cheeks went red. "Oh, no! I'm not related at all," she blurted, a little too fast, and definitely a little too high-pitched.

Calvin's eyes flicked from her to Alex, his eyebrows creeping upward as a grin spread slowly across his face like a cat who'd just discovered the canary was missing from its cage. "Ahhh," he said, dragging the word out. "I get it now. You've got a soft spot for my grandchild, huh? That's what this is about."

Nora's face turned from red to tomato, full-on glowing with the heat of a thousand suns. "No! It's not like that!" she yelped, and somewhere, deep down, wished the floor might just swallow her whole. She glanced at Alex, who was watching the entire scene unfold with an amused, lazy smile, not helping at all. "I mean, Alex is great, but that's really not why I'm here."

Calvin chuckled, a sound that was all good-natured mischief. "Alright, alright," he said, waving his hand in a dismissive but not unfriendly way, like he was brushing off a stray leaf. "Just pulling your leg. But seriously, what's got you poking around in the Turner family history, if it's not romance?"

Nora took a deep breath, trying to regain some semblance of dignity. "I found some old letters at the Majestic Theatre," she said, and once she got going, the words spilled out in a rush, like they'd been waiting for this moment. "They were written by Zeke Turner, and I thought maybe you'd have more letters or something that could help me understand his story."

At the mention of Zeke's name, Calvin's eyes widened, and he broke into a broad smile that made him look twenty years younger. "Zeke Turner, huh? Well now, that's a name I haven't heard in a while. You've got my attention, that's for sure. Come on in, come on in!" He waved them both further into the living room.

Nora, feeling less like an intruder and more like a guest, stepped inside and perched on a well-worn armchair Alex flopped down onto a patchwork-covered couch, still grinning, their body language as easy as someone who had long ago given up on trying to control the chaos of family gatherings. "Grandpa's always been a sucker for a good mystery," Alex said, giving Nora an encouraging nod.

Calvin settled into his own chair. "You're in the right place for family history. Let's see what old Zeke left behind, shall we?"

Nora handed over the letters. She watched as Calvin's face shifted with every passing word—his brow furrowing, his lips twitching, his eyes squinting at the faded handwriting like it was an old friend speaking in code. When he finished, he passed the letters to Alex, who read them with the same intensity.

When the last letter was done, Calvin sat back with a satisfied grin, waving the papers in the air like they were a winning lottery ticket. "Well now, young lady, this is something else! You've hit the goldmine with these letters, no doubt about it. If you've been talking to that librarian, I'm guessing you know what happened to Zeke?"

"Yeah, I found out," she mumbled. "It's awful. He never got the chance to prove he was innocent, and I'm certain he was."

Calvin leaned back, arms folding across his chest as he looked her over again. "Most people would just accept the story they're handed and move on. But you, you're like a dog with a bone, aren't you? I like that."

He leaned forward, dropping his voice into a conspiratorial whisper. "You know, I got interested in all this family history because of a woman at my church. She was doing a podcast series on the histories of black and indigenous people around here. Mighty fine lady, sharp as a tack. If I were thirty years younger... well, I'd be front row at every one of her lectures, that's all I'm saying."

Alex, clearly used to this kind of talk, rolled their eyes and gave their grandfather a light smack on the arm. "Grandpa, behave."

Calvin just chuckled. "What? A man can dream." He turned back to Nora. "Anyway, I dug up some old family letters to help her out, and that's when I found out more about our Zeke. Let's just say the history books only tell half the story."

His tone grew serious now, the playfulness giving way to something more solemn. "There's more to what happened to Zeke than what the newspapers printed. My great-grandfather wrote some things that didn't make it into the official records. I've been keeping them safe for the right time."

With a knowing smile, Calvin reached under his chair and pulled out a small, battered wooden box, the surface scratched and worn from years of use. He opened it carefully, revealing a few yellowed pieces of paper, folded neatly as if they'd been tucked away just yesterday. "Here," he said, handing them over to Nora. "These might fill in some of the blanks. Letters from Zeke's brother, written right around the trial. Not everything made it into the papers, you know."

Nora took the fragile pages from Calvin's hands, the paper crinkling softly beneath her fingers. As she unfolded one letter, the room seemed to hold its breath, a cool breeze brushing past her cheek even though the air was still.

She blinked and shook off the strange sensation, focusing on the letter in her hands. As her eyes moved over the careful handwriting, she felt a slight pressure, almost like a gentle nudge, urging her to continue. Her heart beat a little faster, the room around her seeming to hold its breath.

Dear Brother Zeke,

I pray this letter finds you well. I'm glad to tell you that everything's been arranged for your trip out to the Barbary Coast. Our cousin Elijah has lined up a good spot for you—playing piano at a fine place where folks know good music. He said you're welcome to stay with him and his family when you get there until you get settled on your own. Elijah's word is solid, and I trust you'll find a home out there.

But, brother, I gotta say, it might be best for you and Miss Helen to marry here in Boston before you go.

We don't know what California is like for folks like us, and it's better to have things right before heading out. I found a deacon willing to marry you quietly, without much fuss. I know Miss Helen wanted a Catholic priest, and maybe you can find one in California to do it proper in her church, but this way, you'll be man and wife in the eyes of the Lord.

The deacon is willing to marry you two after the closing night of your show at our church. It'll be quiet, just a few of us, and then you can leave here knowing you've done right by each other.

I want nothing but the best for you, Zeke. You and Helen deserve a chance to build a good life together. Take care, and may God bless this new path you're on.

Your brother,

Samuel

"They never made it that far," Nora sighed, her voice heavy with regret. "She died on opening night."

Calvin nodded, his expression grim. "The letter was in Zeke's personal effects when he was arrested. After he was executed, it went to his next of kin, Samuel. It was never used as evidence in the trial."

"Of course not," Alex scoffed, rolling their eyes. "Why would they bother with evidence when they'd already made up their minds?"

Nora frowned, her fingers tracing the edges of the letter. "How would we even prove he was innocent after so many years?" she wondered aloud.

Calvin leaned back in his chair, stroking his chin. "Well, I suppose we'd have to figure out who actually did it—and gather some kind of evidence."

Nora let out a short, humorless laugh. "That's next to impossible! This all happened over a hundred years ago. Most of the people involved are long gone, and any evidence that existed is probably dust by now."

"I have an idea," Alex interrupted, a spark of excitement in their eyes. "A few months ago, there was a ghost hunting show that did a segment on the Majestic Theatre..."

Nora's eyes widened, her heart skipping a beat. "I saw that! I was so excited when I got the role of Roxie and realized I'd be working in the Majestic!"

Alex nodded. "The medium, Ashlyn Alden, gave me her card. She seemed pretty genuine, as far as mediums go. Maybe she could help us connect with Helen's spirit—or even Zeke's."

"That's brilliant!" Nora exclaimed, leaning forward, her earlier frustration giving way to renewed hope.

Calvin, however, narrowed his eyes. "I don't know about all this ghost stuff. I've never been one to believe in things that go bump in the night. And it's not really proof, anyway."

Alex grinned, patting his arm. "Come on, Grandpa. You've always loved a good mystery. Besides, what have we got to lose? At the very least, it might point us in the right direction."

Calvin huffed. "Well, I suppose it can't hurt to hear what she has to say. But don't expect me to go chasing after ghosts or anything."

Nora smiled, her resolve strengthening. "Alex and I can take care of that. It's settled, then. We'll reach out to Ashlyn and see if she can help us uncover the truth. With her help, maybe we can finally clear Zeke's name and give Helen some peace."

Calvin glanced at Alex, an eyebrow raised. "Since when did you get interested in all this ancestry business?"

"I guess the excitement is just... contagious."

Calvin chuckled and turned back to Nora. "They never cared when it was just me digging around. But a pretty girl shows up, and wham—"

Alex rolled their eyes, but there was a smile tugging at the corners of their mouth.

"Do you have anything else from Samuel or that time period?" Nora asked, knowing that even the smallest piece of information might be helpful.

Calvin shuffled through the papers for a moment before pulling out a small stack of yellowed sheets. "Just these." He handed them to Nora, and she realized it was sheet music—a song titled *My Boston Rose*. As she took the music from him, an overwhelming sense of sadness fell over her, heavy and suffocating, like a damp fog wrapping around her heart. The scent of roses, the one she now associated with Helen, filled her senses. Nora couldn't tell if it was all in her head or if Helen's spirit was there with them, watching over her shoulder.

Nora's knowledge of music was rudimentary, but she recognized the 3/4 time signature on the pages. She could almost see Zeke and Helen waltzing together, lost in a world where their love didn't need to be hidden. As she read through the music, she felt the heart Zeke had put into it and wondered if he had ever had the chance to play it for Helen.

"My Boston Rose" *E. Turner*

(Verse 1) In a theater, bright with splendor, On the stage, she takes her place, With a voice that charms the heavens, And a light that fills the space.

(Chorus) Oh, my Boston Rose, enchanting, How you steal the night away, But our love must stay in shadows, hidden from the light of day.

(Verse 2) When she sings, the world is silent. Every note a whispered plea, But in secret, we find solace, In the love she gives to me.

(Chorus) Oh, my Boston Rose, enchanting, How you steal the night away, But our love must stay in shadows, hidden from the light of day.

(Bridge) Behind the curtain, hearts are racing, In the wings, I watch her shine, Though the world can never see us, Still, I wish that she were mine.

(Verse 3) With each act, she weaves a story, Of a love that cannot be, But beneath her mask of sorrow, Lives the heart she saves for me.

(Chorus) Oh, my Boston Rose, enchanting, How you steal the night away, But our love must stay in shadows, hidden from the light of day.

(Outro) In the glow of footlights burning, And the final curtain's fall, I will wait there in the darkness, Till she hears my silent call.

Nora put the pages down, blinking back tears. "It's beautiful," she whispered.

Alex moved closer and placed a hand on her shoulder. Nora felt a jolt, like the tiniest spark of static. She bit her lip and looked away, unable to meet their eyes. Alex was so sure of themself, so steady—how could they ever be interested in someone as tangled and awkward as her?

"I can play it," Alex said, their voice low.

"Alex is a brilliant musician and performer," Calvin interjected. He sprang up and began shoving stacks of books and papers off an old table. Except, of course, it wasn't a table at all—it was a piano, buried under the detritus of a thousand forgotten afternoons.

Once the piano was revealed, Calvin gave a theatrical bow and gestured for Alex to take a seat. Alex accepted the sheet music from Nora, their fingers brushing hers, sending another jolt up her arm. They sat down at the piano and then began to play.

The music filled the room, and Nora felt it wrap around her, soft and insistent. Alex's voice joined the melody, deep and smoky, each note tugging at something deep inside her chest. She wondered, not for the first time, what it would be like to be Helen, and if Alex was anything like Zeke. She shook her head, clearing the silly thoughts away, but her heart wouldn't quite let go of the idea.

When the last notes faded into silence, Nora realized she had been holding her breath. She let it out in a rush, then stammered, "I think it's you who should be on the stage."

Alex gave her a small, crooked smile. "Thank you," they said, but their voice was wistful. "There was a time when I wanted that more than anything. I love the theater, but the roles... well, there aren't a lot of them for someone like me. Like when people ask my vocal range. Do I say contralto? Countertenor? It's all a bit much sometimes." They laughed, but it was a brittle sound.

Nora had never seen Alex like this—so uncertain, so... *unguarded*. They seemed like the calm in any storm, the one who never flinched, no matter what chaos surrounded them. But standing here now, she could see the cracks, the places where their usual confidence didn't quite reach. It was a strange, quiet reminder that even the most self-assured people weren't as invincible as they seemed. It made her think about herself—how many times had she thrown on a smile or some forced bravado when, inside; she felt anything but steady? How much of Alex's confidence was real, and how much was armor?

She stepped closer, her heart doing a little flip as she hesitated before laying her hand over theirs. The contact was solid but trembling beneath the surface, like a string pulled too tight. Their fingers stiffened under her touch, and for a moment, she wasn't sure if it was helping or just making it worse. The vulnerability in that moment sent a shiver through her.

Alex looked up at her, their eyes searching hers, and for a moment, they just sat there, hand in hand, connected by the quiet understanding that sometimes, being strong meant showing the places where you weren't.

Just as the silence wrapped around them, Calvin clapped his hands, jolting them both back to reality.

"Well! That was a heart-wrenching display of vulnerability," he declared with a dramatic flourish. "If I had a heart, it'd be weeping right now. But let's save the theatrics for later—there's a mystery afoot!"

"Right," Alex said, clearing their throat and sitting up straighter. "We need to focus. There has to be evidence somewhere, and we need to prove Zeke's innocence. I'll reach out to Ashlyn."

"What should I do?" Nora asked, standing up, her mind snapping back to the task at hand.

"One letter mentioned a Pritchard and another actress," Alex said. "Maybe you can dig up more about them?"

Nora nodded, making a mental note. "Will you let me know what the medium says?"

"Of course." Alex held out their hand. "Give me your phone."

Nora blinked, but handed her phone over. Alex typed in their number and texted themself. "There—we've got each other's numbers now."

Nora blushed. "See you at rehearsal on Monday?" she asked.

Alex nodded with a smile. "Can't wait!"

CHAPTER SIX

Intermission

Nora opened the door to her apartment with gusto, the handle rattling in protest as she threw herself inside. She was on cloud nine! Her class today had been a blast—the preschool kids were growing on her. Sure, they were a little loud and had the attention spans of hummingbirds, but they were sweet and enthusiastic, and their excitement for dance was infectious.

And Linda had solidified her plans for the Musical Theater intensive—Fosse-themed, no less! It was a dream come true for Nora, who was a big fan of the legendary choreographer's sultry, stylized moves. Alex had called yesterday, and just thinking about their voice made Nora's heart flutter all over again. They'd confirmed that Ashlyn Alden would come to the Majestic Theatre after rehearsal. Tonight!

She still couldn't quite believe it—*the* Ashlyn Alden, who was a guest on all the best paranormal shows, was going to help them connect with the spirits in the theater. The real Ashlyn Alden! She glanced over at the tin of letters on her desk, the ones she'd discovered hidden in the theater. "We'll figure out what happened, Helen," she whispered, her fingers brushing the cool metal of the tin. The room seemed to hold its breath in response, as if the very walls were listening.

She didn't even bother changing out of her leotard and leggings. Instead, she just threw on a T-shirt over them. Tonight's rehearsal was a small one, just her and Ciera, focusing on "Nowadays/Hot Honey Rag." They would dance—really dance, with all the flair and finesse that the number required.

She bounced on her toes, feeling like she might burst from happiness. Mondays usually had a reputation for being the worst day of the week, but whoever came up with that hadn't had a day like hers. Today was shaping up to be perfect, and she couldn't wait to see what else it had in store.

As she headed toward the Majestic, Nora's mind drifted to Alex and the strange, fluttery feelings that seemed to take over whenever she thought of them. She'd always put her dance career first—everything else came second, including relationships. Sure, she'd gone on a few dates here and there, but they usually ended with some guy who was more interested in how flexible she was than in who she was as a person.

But Alex was different. They weren't anything like those men, who only pretended to be charming until they slipped up and said something gross. No, Alex was kind and funny and—Nora's cheeks flushed hot, and she ducked her head, trying to hide her smile from no one in particular—smooth. That voice of theirs could melt butter, and they had this way of making her feel like she was the only person in the room. She was looking forward to seeing them more than she cared to admit, even to herself.

Her cheeks were still red as she walked into the theater, and lo-and-behold—there was Alex, standing right by the entrance, waiting for her.

"Hey," they said, flashing a smile that could break her heart into a million tiny pieces and still leave her wanting more.

"Hi yourself," she replied, aiming for flirty but landing somewhere between awkward and tongue-tied. Her blush deepened, spreading all the way to her ears, but if Alex noticed, they didn't show it.

Instead, they stepped forward and wrapped her in a hug. "I just wanted to say hi before you got caught up in rehearsal. I'm excited about ghost hunting with you tonight."

"Me too," Nora said, hugging them back and wishing she didn't have to let go. It was a wonderful hug, the kind that made her feel like she belonged there, safe and sound. But then, of course, her brain ruined it with that pesky inner voice. *What if they don't really like you? What if they're just this nice to everyone?*

She took a step back, trying to shake off her doubts. Alex, thankfully, didn't seem to notice the turmoil brewing inside her. They both stood there in silence for a moment, and just when it got a little too quiet, Nora found her voice. "I'll see you after rehearsal?"

Alex nodded, still smiling. "I'll see you during!" they said with a grin.

Today's rehearsal was being led by the choreographer. The only performers in the building were herself, Ciera, and Lexi, which should have made things easier, but somehow only made everything worse. Lexi was now understudying both Velma and Roxie, and from the way her feet kept tangling up under her, she was having a terrible time of it. They had already learned the music, but translating notes into steps was proving more difficult than any of them had expected.

Lexi fumbled her way through the routine, her movements awkward and offbeat. Nora felt a twinge of sympathy watching her, but it was hard to hold on to with that small, sneaky flicker of relief creeping in. Martin's sigh of frustration echoed across the stage, but this time, it wasn't aimed at her. For once, she wasn't the one under the spotlight, messing up. She didn't want to smile, but there it was—just a tiny one, barely noticeable.

Nora hovered near the back, doing her best to stay out of the line of fire, while Lexi tried to juggle two sets of choreography at once. It was like watching a duck try to waltz—her legs tangled up beneath her as she fumbled through the steps. Poor Lexi, Nora thought, feeling guilty for enjoying the chaos. She knew how it felt to be the one in the spotlight, tripping over her own feet and Martin's constant corrections.

Ciera, who was usually perfect, seemed to wrestle with the choreography too. Her brow furrowed, and her face twisted in confusion, as if someone had swapped out her feet when she wasn't looking. This was new—Ciera was normally unflappable, gliding through every step with the grace of a swan. Today, though, she looked lost.

Martin, meanwhile, looked like he was about to combust as he watched the choreographer clapping her hands and barking out counts like a drill sergeant. He paced back and forth, muttering under his breath about timing and technique, his face growing redder by the second. Nora couldn't help the little bubble of satisfaction that rose. It was a rare day when she wasn't the one making Martin's eyebrows do that dangerous twitching thing. She kept her head down, steps precise. It was a minor victory, but in a sea of rehearsals where she usually felt like a floundering fish, it felt downright triumphant.

She glanced over to see Alex marking the movements well—too well, in fact. That sneaky little performer. They were a dancer too! Effortlessly moving with a kind of casual grace suggested they were having no trouble at all. Even adding extra flair to their steps that were almost obnoxious in its smoothness. They looked up and noticed Nora watching, but instead of being embarrassed, they gave her a wink and threw in a cheeky little spin.

Nora giggled, which drew Martin's exasperated gaze. "Nora, honey," he said, rolling his eyes, "it's gonna be a bit. Why don't you take a quick break so I don't murder you..."

She gave him a sheepish smile and nodded, slipping off to the side to catch her breath. For once, it wasn't her fault things were going awry, and she intended to savor every minute.

Alex sauntered over with a bottle of water and handed it to Nora, their smile easy and warm. She took the bottle, sucking down half of it in one go and wiping her mouth with the back of her hand, trying not to think about how sweaty she must look. "Thanks," she said, smiling back, trying to ignore the way her pulse quickened whenever Alex was around.

"Anytime," they replied. "You're in your element tonight." They reached out and brushed a stray piece of hair from her eyes. The subtle, lingering contact sent a shiver down her spine, and Nora's heart did a funny little flip. She knew she was grinning like an idiot, but she couldn't help it. There was something about Alex—something that made the universe tilt sideways and turn bright and strange.

"Do you think we'll connect Helen, or any spirits, tonight?" she blurted out, regretting it. It wasn't the smoothest line, but it was something. After all, everyone knew the theater had its fair share of ghost stories.

The Majestic was infamous for them. There were tales of cold spots and strange noises, of props that moved on their own and mirrors that showed reflections of people who weren't there. Once, someone had even claimed to see a figure on the balcony, watching with dark, hollow eyes.

Alex didn't laugh, though. Instead, they seemed to consider the question, tilting their head to the side in that way they did when they were deep in thought. "Hmm," they murmured. "Well, if not Helen or Zeke, there's always the rumor about the old stagehand who still haunts the place, looking for his lost toolbox. And then there's the story about the actor who never quite left her dressing room. They say he still paces back and forth, muttering his lines. Sometimes, if you're quiet, you can hear whispering in the walls."

Nora shivered, but not from the thought of ghosts. There was something enchanting about the way Alex spoke, like they were weaving a spell with their words. She leaned in closer, drawn to them and hanging on every word. She was about to ask them for more ghostly gossip when Martin's voice cut through the air like a knife.

"Nora—break's up! Let's run this thing!" he called from across the stage.

Nora gave Alex one last lingering look, her stomach doing another little flip. "Guess I better get back to it," she said, pulling away. Alex's smile was soft, almost knowing, as if they could see right through her.

"Break a leg," they said, their voice low and warm, and Nora felt her cheeks heat as she turned back toward the stage. She tried to shake off the silly, fluttery feeling and focus. But as she headed back to her spot, she couldn't help but glance over her shoulder, just in time to see Alex watching back, and her heart skipped a beat all over again.

After everyone else had gone and the echoes of footsteps had faded into silence, Martin approached them. "You good to lock up, kiddo?" he asked Alex, his voice gruff. Alex gave a nod, and Martin gathered his things, turning back one more time with a crooked smile. "You crazy kids have fun tonight. And don't do anything I wouldn't do!"

"So, do whatever we want?" Alex shot back.

Martin just grunted in response and shuffled out the door, leaving the theater for the two of them.

Nora couldn't help but feel a little jealous of the straightforward relationship Alex had with Martin. The older man still terrified her a bit, with his barked orders and his furrowed brow. "How are you able to talk to him like that?" she asked as they sat alone in the empty theater, the vastness of the space making her voice sound smaller than usual. Ashlyn had yet to arrive, and the quiet was almost eerie, like the building was holding its breath.

Alex leaned back in their chair, a small smile playing on their lips. "I practically grew up here," they said. "My dad was a lighting tech, and I loved the theater from the moment I first set foot in it. He'd drag me along to work with him, let me watch the shows from the spot booth. Eventually, I got to work the spotlight myself."

"That sounds amazing! Does your dad still do lights?" Nora asked.

Alex's smile faltered, a hint of sadness creeping into their eyes. "He died when I was thirteen."

"Oh, I'm so sorry," Nora said, reaching out without thinking and touching their face. She froze, realizing what she'd done, but Alex just placed a hand over hers, holding it there. She felt a warmth spread through her, a soft, comforting heat that settled, making her feel all warm and gooey inside.

"Thanks," Alex murmured, squeezing her hand before letting go. "It was right in the middle of a rough spot in my life. My dad always got me, you know? My mom, not so much. Martin was a lifesaver back then. He always said that theater folk take care of their own. I started working as a grip around that time, and I've been at the Majestic ever since."

Nora smiled, touched by the story. "That's beautiful. Your mom, is she..." she trailed off, realizing she was venturing into dangerous territory.

Alex laughed, a soft sound that eased some of the tension in the room. "She's alive and well. Grandpa Calvin is her dad. We don't talk much these days, though." Their lips thinned, and Nora noted the flicker of pain in their eyes. This was not a subject they wanted to dwell on.

Nora let it go, sensing that some things were better left unsaid. Instead, she reached out and gave Alex's hand a gentle squeeze. The theater was still and quiet around them, and for a moment, it felt like they were the only two people in the world.

"Tell me more about the theater ghosts," Nora said, breaking the silence.

Alex's face lit up. "Calvin doesn't think I like history, but that's not true." They grinned, their excitement contagious. "I just like the little bits no one ever hears about. The *human* stuff, you know?"

Nora leaned in, smiling. She could tell this was going to be good.

"When Ashlyn's crew came in to film that documentary," Alex continued, warming to the topic, "I was *so* excited to be the tech on site. They had historians digging up all kinds of stuff about this place. Like Edward

Pritchard—one of the suspected haunts. His family were major benefactors when the theater was built."

"Oh, I did some research on him on Sunday," Nora said, glancing at Alex.

"Yeah? What did you find?"

Nora leaned in, her voice lowering. "Turns out, he was known for his predatory behavior—specifically around the theater. His family poured a lot of money into this place, and he expected people to worship him for it."

"That tracks. You can still feel the creepiness lingering here," Alex said. "It's like his influence left a stain. He had this... reputation. Not just for getting what he wanted, but for making sure people feared him."

"Did you find anything on the understudy?" Alex prompted.

"Catherine Mayfield," Nora said. "I came across a few mentions of her. Let's just say, she might've had a similar... dynamic with Pritchard as Helen did."

"Interesting," Alex replied, frowning in thought. "I don't remember anything about her from Ashlyn's crew, but there were a lot of names to sift through. They focused on the spirits that manifested."

Nora's voice softened. "Helen and Zeke?"

"Helen's tied to this place," Alex said, their tone more thoughtful now. "But Zeke... not so much. Records for black musicians back then were often incomplete, or missing altogether, especially if they weren't famous. The system didn't care enough to remember them. He didn't die here, either, so there's less connection."

"Oh," Nora replied. Zeke had come to life for her through the letters—passionate, full of humanity. It felt wrong that his legacy could be lost while Helen's remained intact.

Alex gave her a sympathetic look, sensing her thoughts. "Yeah," they said. "It's messed up how easily people like Zeke got erased. But Calvin's done his best to keep our family story alive."

Alex must've sensed the shift because they changed gears. "There's also Ollie, you met him. He likes to scream during performances. It's hilarious."

Nora's eyebrows shot up. "During a production?"

"Yup," Alex said, grinning. "Throws a lot of the actors. The audience always thinks it's just someone's kid, so they get all annoyed. We usually leave a stuffed toy on an empty seat just to keep the little guy entertained."

Nora giggled. "Thanks for the heads up!"

"Of course," Alex replied, leaning forward to brush a stray piece of hair from Nora's face. Her heart raced at the gesture, a flutter of nerves and excitement.

Their eyes met again, and this time, Nora couldn't help but inhale. She leaned forward, her pulse quickening as Alex's lips parted—

"Hello?" Ashlyn Alden's voice echoed through the theater, carrying with it a kind of warm authority that caught Nora's attention.

A woman with dark hair and a long, flowing skirt wandered down the aisle, moving with a casual grace that made it hard to look away. At first glance, there was nothing out of the ordinary about her—just dark hair that spilled over her shoulders and striking eyes. But there was something more to Ashlyn Alden. It wasn't her beauty, though she had a unique, almost otherworldly elegance. It was her *presence*. She radiated warmth and strength in a way that made you feel you'd been wrapped in your favorite old blanket, the kind you keep because it smells like home. No wonder the ghosts were drawn to her.

Ashlyn embraced Alex with an easy familiarity, kissing them on both cheeks. On anyone else, it might have looked pretentious, the gesture you see people do at fancy parties where no one really knows each other. But with Ashlyn, it was as natural as breathing, like she'd been doing it her whole life and everyone loved her for it.

"This is Nora Sinclair," Alex said, turning to introduce her. "And Nora, this is Ashlyn Alden."

Nora froze, her heart stumbling like it had tripped over its own feet. *Ashlyn Alden.* The Ashlyn Alden. The one from all those ghost-hunting shows she binge-watched on rainy afternoons, wrapped in a blanket with a mug of tea. She'd imagined meeting her a hundred times, and now here she was. Of course, in her head, she'd been witty and charming, saying something clever that Ashlyn would laugh at, maybe even nod approvingly. But in reality? She could only manage a nervous smile, the kind that said, *Hi, I'm completely overwhelmed and possibly about to embarrass myself.*

Ashlyn didn't seem to notice Nora's internal panic. She stepped forward with that same welcoming energy and pulled Nora into a hug. Normally, Nora would have cringed at the unexpected closeness—physical affection from strangers was not her thing—but with Ashlyn, it was... fine. More than fine. It felt almost comforting.

"And now," Ashlyn said, stepping back and clapping her hands, "tell me what we know, and what we're hoping to learn."

Nora glanced at Alex, who gave her an encouraging nod, and together they explained everything: the love letters between Helen and Zeke, Zeke's trial and conviction for Helen's murder, and that Zeke was one of Alex's ancestors.

Ashlyn listened, her head tilted as if she were absorbing not just the facts but the emotions woven through them. When Nora mentioned Zeke's conviction, Ashlyn's brow furrowed in thought, but when Alex revealed their family connection to him, Ashlyn's eyes lit up with sudden interest.

"Oh, that could be helpful," she mused, her voice low and thoughtful. "Do you have the letters?"

Nora reached into her bag and pulled out the box of letters. As she handed them to Ashlyn, the psychic's fingers brushed hers, and a shiver ran down Nora's spine. It wasn't an unpleasant feeling, but it left her oddly exposed, like Ashlyn could see straight through her.

Ashlyn paused, her gaze lingering on Nora for just a moment longer than expected. "You have a gift, you know," she breathed.

Nora blinked, surprised. "A gift?"

Ashlyn nodded. "You're more receptive to spirits than most people. You may not realize it, but you can feel things others can't—see things they overlook. It's almost more of an empathic ability."

Nora's heart skipped a beat. "What does that mean? Is it... safe?"

Ashlyn smiled, her eyes softening with reassurance. "Oh, it's perfectly safe. What you're experiencing is a natural sensitivity. Spirits—especially ones with unfinished business—are drawn to people like you because you can understand them in ways others can't. It might explain why you feel such a strong connection to Helen."

Ashlyn reached out and squeezed Nora's hand. "If you ever feel like it's a burden, or if it overwhelms you, you can reach out to me. I'll help you manage it."

Nora exhaled. "Okay," she whispered. "Thank you."

Ashlyn acknowledged her with a gentle smile and opened the tin as if it were something sacred. She sifted through the letters.

"What's our goal?" Ashlyn asked, her fingers pausing over the fragile edges of a letter.

"We want to prove Zeke's innocence," Alex said. "If it's possible."

Ashlyn nodded, her expression shifting to something more serious, more focused. "All right," she said. "Let's see what we can do."

"Where do you want to start?" Alex asked as they walked toward the stage.

"Up here is good," Ashlyn replied.

"I'll go get the lights."

Alex bounded off as Nora watched. They had such a beautiful love for life. The stage lights came. Alex dragged a few folding of chairs to the stage, placing them in the center. As Ashlyn prepared to commune with the spirits, the stage was quiet, save for the soft rustle of fabric as she moved. Alex and Nora sat in folding chairs positioned near the center of the stage, each waiting in silence. A third chair sat empty, ready for Ashlyn when the time came.

Ashlyn moved almost reverently across the stage, her steps soft and deliberate. She wasn't in a rush—this wasn't something to be hurried. She was feeling the space, testing the energy. Now and then, she would pause, closing her eyes for a moment, as if listening to something no one else could hear.

The dim theater lights cast long shadows that seemed to stretch across the stage, adding a weight to the air. The room, already vast and echoing, seemed to grow more still. Ashlyn walked to the far end of the stage and stood for a long moment, facing out toward the empty seats. Her hands rested at her sides, but her posture was calm, grounded. Everything about her said *presence*. She was waiting, but for what? Nora wasn't sure.

Without warning, a chill swept through the room, sharp and sudden. The temperature dropped in an instant, the cool air raising goosebumps on Nora's arms. She inhaled, her body tensing. It wasn't just cold—it was a cold that seemed to seep into her bones, bringing with it an overwhelming sense of dread. She didn't move, didn't speak, but her heart hammered, an icy trickle of fear crawling up her spine. The stage, which had felt like a sanctuary moments before, now seemed like a place she didn't want to be.

Out of instinct, Nora turned her head toward Alex, seeking comfort in their presence. To her surprise, Alex was already looking at her, their eyes wide with something that mirrored what she was feeling. The fear. The *knowing* that something was here. Alex's usual calm had vanished, replaced by a flicker of unease that they were trying—and failing—to hide.

Neither of them said a word. They both just sat there, gripping the edges of their chairs, as the cold pressed down on them like an invisible weight.

Ashlyn seemed unfazed by the change, or perhaps she had expected it. She approached the empty chair, the stage floor creaking beneath her feet, and took her place in the center of the two. The temperature had already shifted, the air around them thick with tension. Ashlyn sat straight, eyes closed for a moment, hands resting on her lap, composed despite the atmosphere that had changed.

Nora bit her lip, keeping quiet, though her mind raced. Her fear was almost tangible now, but something in her trusted Ashlyn—this was part of the process, wasn't it?

She glanced at Alex again, who gave her the smallest of nods, as if to say, *Stay steady*. They were both holding it together, but only just.

Ashlyn opened her eyes and spoke out loud. "If there are any spirits present, we're here to listen." Her voice carried through the stillness, calm and welcoming. "We come with respect."

The silence that followed felt deep, like the theater itself was holding its breath. The air was thick, as if time had slowed to a crawl, every creak of the old stage and faint shuffle of feet amplified in the stillness. Ashlyn sat still, eyes closed, her brow furrowing with concentration. She seemed... strained, like she was trying to tune into something just out of reach.

"There are so many voices," she murmured. "All trying to speak... reaching for Helen."

The words sent a shiver down Nora's spine, and she swallowed hard, her eyes darting around the stage. The shadows felt heavier now, stretching long, as if the theater itself was shifting under unseen forces. Nora shifted in her chair, very aware of how exposed they were in the middle of the stage.

Ashlyn's eyes snapped open, darting around the space, scanning it as if she could *see* something—something neither Nora nor Alex could.

The lights overhead flickered, casting the stage in a stuttering, eerie glow. A faint buzz filled the air, like the hum of electricity straining against the theater's old wiring. The hum grew louder, a high-pitched whine that made the back of Nora's teeth ache.

Nora glanced at Alex. "Is this... normal?"

Alex shook their head, eyes wide, lips pressed into a tight line. "No," they whispered.

Before Nora could ask another question, the theater itself seemed to answer. A deep, guttural groan rumbled through the walls, so low it felt like it came from the foundation—like the very bones of the place were protesting under some unseen weight. It was the sound that made your teeth ache, the sound that warned of things shifting in the dark.

Then came the screech.

Metal, twisting, slow and deliberate, like nails dragging across a chalkboard, but far worse. It scraped through the air, and Nora's breath hitched, her heart stuttering. She tilted her head back, eyes wide, just in time to see it—the massive lighting rig overhead shifting. Not by much, just a whisper of movement, but enough to make the lights sway, as if something unseen had given them a nudge.

"Alex..." Nora whispered.

The groaning grew louder, more insistent, vibrating through the floor beneath their feet. Alex shot to their feet, eyes wide with alarm. "Nora, MOVE!"

The shout cut through the air. but Nora was frozen, rooted to the spot. Then Alex was moving, crossing the space in a heartbeat, their hands gripping Nora's shoulders in a bruising grip as they yanked her sideways. The world tilted, her feet scrambling to keep up, when—

CRACK.

A stage light broke free, crashing down with a thunderous bang, smashing into the chair where Nora had been sitting. Shards of metal and glass exploded outward, the sound reverberating through the empty theater like a gunshot. The force of it sent a shudder up through the floor, rattling Nora's bones as she staggered back, gasping for breath.

But before she could process the narrow escape, something else groaned—a deeper, more ominous noise. This time, it wasn't coming from the rig.

It was coming from the walls.

Chapter Seven

Act 2

"What *is* that?" Nora breathed. The ringing in her ears was fading, and she realized it wasn't real—just the echo of her pulse pounding in her head. Her gaze was still locked on the shattered remains of the chair, now a mangled mess of splinters and crushed metal. The stage light that had crashed down was sprawled out like some twisted, broken beast, its cables curling across the floor like dead serpents.

Alex was already pulling Nora to her feet, eyes darting toward the ceiling, checking to make sure nothing else was about to fall. "Are you okay?" they asked, voice tight, sharp with adrenaline.

Nora nodded, though her heart was still hammering. "Yeah. I think so." She glanced at the wreckage again, her skin crawling with the realization of how close it had been. If Alex hadn't moved her, if they'd been just a second slower—

"Everyone in one piece?" Alex's voice cut through her spiraling thoughts, steadying her. They turned, eyes scanning the room until they landed on Ashlyn, who was still sitting, serene amid the chaos.

Ashlyn's gaze was distant, her eyes following something none of them could see. "That was a warning," she murmured, her voice as cold as a winter draft. The calm way she said it, like she'd been expecting it, made a shiver trace down Nora's spine. It was as if the crash was the exclamation point at the end of some unseen conversation.

"A warning?" Alex repeated, incredulous. "Ashlyn, that light nearly *killed* someone!"

Ashlyn blinked, finally shifting her gaze to the others. "Helen wants to speak," she said, her tone unwavering. "But someone—or something—doesn't want her to."

Nora swallowed hard, her mind racing. The scent of roses still hung in the air, as though the theater itself was breathing around them, alive and full of secrets. "Helen is here?"

Ashlyn nodded, her face pale but composed. "She's trying to reach out. There's something she needs to say, something unfinished." Her gaze flicked toward the crumpled stage light, lips pressed into a thin line. "But she's not the only one here."

The silence that followed was thick and suffocating, broken only by the faint creak of the theater settling around them. Nora's skin prickled as if something—or someone—was watching, waiting in the wings, just out of sight.

Alex let out a breath, running a hand through their hair. "Alright, so what do we do? If the lights are going to start dropping, we can't just—"

Before they could finish, a soft sound echoed through the space—a sigh, low and mournful. It seemed to come from nowhere and everywhere all at once. The three of them froze, listening, hearts pounding in unison.

"What was that?" Nora whispered.

Ashlyn stood, her eyes scanning the dim corners of the room. "It's Helen," she said, her tone matter-of-fact, as if she'd been expecting this all along. "But she's not alone." She stepped forward, her presence somehow grounding, even in the eerie quiet.

Alex's eyes darted toward the darkened backstage, their body tense. "We need to get out of here," they muttered. "Or at least figure out who—or *what*—is trying to kill us before it drops the whole stage on our heads."

Nora's breath caught as a cold breeze swept through the theater, carrying with it the unmistakable scent of roses. The lights overhead flickered once, twice, casting long shadows that seemed to stretch and writhe across the walls like living things. They dimmed, and this time, the shadow of a woman appeared on the far side of the stage, barely there, as if made of smoke and whispers. It lingered for a moment, watching, waiting—and then it vanished.

Ashlyn's gaze locked with Nora's, her expression sharper than it had been moments before. "Helen wants to tell her story," she said, voice low, "but we need somewhere safe."

Alex shot her a look, eyebrows raised. "Somewhere *safe*? What does that even mean?"

Ashlyn gave them a glance that was somewhere between patient and exasperated, like she was explaining to a child why fire is hot. She turned back to Nora. "Where did you first find her?"

Nora shifted on her feet. "I never really *met* her," she admitted. "But I found her journal. I can show you."

Ashlyn tilted her head, considering. "Lead the way."

They moved through the winding corridors, the air thick with the smell of dust and time. Alex kept pace, mentioning that the storage room had once been a dressing room, though the walls held more than just mirrors and costumes now.

Nora stopped in front of a faded seam in the wall, her hand brushing over the rough surface. "It was here," she said softly, her voice almost swallowed by the shadows. "This is where I found it."

Ashlyn's eyes followed Nora's hand, but her focus was elsewhere—her head tilted, as if listening to something just out of reach.

"I could always smell roses," Nora added. "Whenever I read the journal."

Ashlyn pulled the cushy chair over to the far wall, and for a moment, it was as though the room remembered itself. The dusty corners softened, and Nora could almost see it as it had been—glamorous in a faded way. A mirror with a row of lights flickering above it, a makeup table cluttered with powders and brushes. It was easy to picture Helen sitting there, preparing for her performance, oblivious to the tragedy that was to come.

Ashlyn sat down, shutting her eyes, her body swaying. The air in the room felt thicker somehow, like it was waiting.

"What's happening?" Nora whispered, the hairs on the back of her neck rising.

Ashlyn's hand shot up, palm outward, a silent plea for quiet. The swaying grew more pronounced, her breath coming in sharp, shallow gasps. Then her entire body went rigid. A low, guttural sound escaped her—a grunt, full of anger and pain, followed by a soft, pitiful whimper that made Nora's skin crawl.

Nora glanced at Alex, panic flashing in her eyes. *Should they help her?* She didn't know what was happening, didn't know what to do. Alex looked just as uncertain, their fingers twitching like they wanted to intervene but weren't sure how. So they both stood, frozen, as the temperature in the room dipped, their breath coming out in faint puffs of mist.

And then, as quickly as it began, it was over. Ashlyn slumped forward in the chair, her body shaking off the tension like a bird ruffling its feathers. She stood, her face pale and drawn, but her eyes clear.

"I'm so sorry," she said. "I should've explained better. Helen wanted to show me what happened, and I—I didn't prepare you." She took a step toward them, arms open. "It's kind of like... reliving her death. It's terrifying, but you get used to it. I've done it enough times that I can shed the trauma afterward. I didn't mean to scare you."

Before either of them could respond, she pulled them into a tight hug, warm despite the cold that still lingered in the air. Nora felt herself relax against Ashlyn, though her mind still raced.

Nora's chest tightened as Alex pulled back, rubbing the back of their neck in that awkward, nervous way that made them seem both relatable and, for some reason, reassuring. "Did you..." Alex trailed off, the unspoken question hanging between them.

"...see what happened?" Nora finished, her voice quieter, as if speaking too loud might make the moment unravel.

Their eyes met, and for a brief, absurd second, they both giggled. It wasn't the kind of laugh that came from humor, more the kind that bursts out when tension coils so tight inside you that it has to find an escape somewhere. The kind of laugh that says, *we're still alive, right?*

Ashlyn raised an eyebrow, the corner of her mouth twitching into a knowing grin, like she'd seen this all before—people, shaken by something unspeakable, trying to patch themselves back together with nervous smiles. She'd seen enough, no doubt, to know what that felt like.

"I did," she said, her voice steady, but her eyes... her eyes were somewhere else.

Nora felt her stomach drop. Something about the way her face clouded, as if she were dragging herself through the memory, made Nora's skin prickle with dread.

"It's like being inside someone else's skin," Ashlyn began, her tone soft but clear. "Helen was getting ready for the evening's performance. You could feel her excitement—like an electric hum just beneath the surface. She thought it was going to be a good night."

The room seemed to darken, not literally, but in that way where the air thickens and every little noise fades into the background. The sound of traffic outside, the distant hum of the building, all of it receded, leaving only Ashlyn's voice to fill the space.

"She was brushing her hair, humming to herself," Ashlyn continued, and Nora could almost see it—the soft glow of a vanity mirror, Helen's reflection looking back with that quiet smile people wear when they're thinking of someone they love. "Then there was a knock at the door. She thought it was him—Zeke. Her heart jumped. You could feel it, the way everything in her lit up with anticipation."

Nora's pulse quickened, and she glanced at Alex, who was leaning in, just as caught in Ashlyn's words as she was.

"But when she opened the door..." Ashlyn's voice dipped lower, more haunted. "...it wasn't Zeke. It was a man—tall, thin, with skin stretched too tight over his bones. His eyes were dark, hollow, like he was already halfway to something terrible. He smiled and handed her flowers."

Nora's mouth went dry, a creeping unease snaking up her spine. Ashlyn's description painted the scene, Nora could almost smell the musty, overripe scent of the flowers in the man's hands.

"Something about the way he did it," Ashlyn's voice faltered for a moment, "made her skin crawl. But she accepted them. What else could she do?"

Nora's breath hitched as Ashlyn's fingers curled into her palms, tension rippling through the room like a sudden gust of cold air.

"Then... he stepped closer. Too close." Ashlyn's face tightened, her voice carrying what was coming next. "He grabbed her, put his mouth on hers, and she shoved him back. She was scared—*really* scared now. But he didn't stop. His smile twisted, turned ugly. He wanted more."

The words hung in the air like a terrible fog. Nora's stomach churned, her hands balling into fists at her sides. The room seemed colder, heavier. She could feel Helen's fear like a cold hand on her shoulder, like it was seeping through the walls of the theater, wrapping around her.

"They struggled," Ashlyn's voice shook, but she kept going. "She scratched at his arms, tried to scream, but he slammed her against the table. The corner hit her head. Hard."

Nora felt her breath catch, her mind conjuring the image before she could stop it—Helen crumpling to the floor, the brutal, hollow sound of her body hitting wood.

"Not dead," Ashlyn said "Just... unconscious."

Nora's heart was racing now, her eyes wide, waiting for the next horrible thing that she already knew was coming. But hearing it... *hearing* it from Ashlyn made it feel like it was happening right in front of her.

"The man panicked," Ashlyn continued, her voice growing tight. "He turned to leave, but then—" she hesitated, her brow furrowing as if pushing through the memory herself "—he came back. He couldn't help himself. His hands wrapped around her throat. He squeezed, tighter and tighter."

Nora's throat felt like it was closing up, her breath shallow as she listened, her hands trembling in her lap.

"And then—" Ashlyn's fingers twitched, mimicking the sound of a sharp crack. Her own voice trembled, just a little. "Her neck snapped."

A shiver ran through the room, cold and sharp. Nora swallowed hard, her heart pounding so loud she was sure Alex could hear it. The air was too thick, too cold.

She felt sick, like the world had tilted just a bit too far off its axis.

"And then?" Alex's voice was a whisper, but somehow it cut through the dense silence like a knife.

Ashlyn's face paled, her eyes hollow as she spoke. "He scurried away, like a rat in the dark, but before he could escape, someone came down the hall." She paused, her voice tightening with disgust. "He ran right into Zeke. And that's when his fear turned... cruel. He pointed back at the room, right at Helen's body, and screamed, 'Murder most foul!' He tried to frame Zeke for what he had done."

Nora gasped, her hands shaking now. Everything about the story clawed at her, the injustice, the horror, the sheer wrongness of it all.

With fumbling fingers, she pulled out her phone. Her stomach flipped as she scrolled to a picture she'd snapped in the lobby earlier that week. *It couldn't be.* But it had to be.

She turned the screen toward Ashlyn. "Did the man... look like this?" Her voice was shaking as she showed the image: a portrait of Edward Pritchard, the theater's benefactor.

Ashlyn's breath hitched, her face going pale. Her hand trembled as she reached for the phone, her eyes locking onto the image. She didn't speak at first, but the look on her face said it all.

"Yes," she breathed, her face ashen. "That's him."

Nora felt the world sway beneath her, her stomach lurching as if she were falling through the floor. Everything made sense now, and yet none of it did.

Before any of them could speak, a soft sound broke the silence—a slow, deliberate *footstep* in the hallway. Then another. The air seemed to freeze in place, the shadows stretching and deepening as the sound grew closer, each footfall echoing through the old walls like a distant drumbeat.

Nora's pulse quickened, her eyes darting to Alex, then to Ashlyn.

The footsteps stopped just outside the door.

The temperature dropped, sharp and sudden, like stepping into a winter's breath. It wasn't just cold—it was the kind of chill that crept under your skin, burrowed into your bones. Nora shivered, her breath coming out in small puffs of mist. The air thickened, pressing against them, making it hard to breathe.

Ashlyn stiffened, her eyes wide as if she could see something none of them could—a shadow moving just beyond the edge of the light, circling them. The room felt tight, the walls too close, the space shrinking behind something unseen.

Then it hit. A force, raw and invisible, slammed into them like a wave. Alex moved without thinking, stepping between Nora and the assault, but the air itself seemed to coil around them, twisting, tightening. The cold deepened, and the lights flickered, casting jagged shadows that crawled up the walls like broken fingers.

Nora's skin crawled with a prickling dread. She didn't need to see it to know—it was there. *He* was there. Something old, something wrong, like the feeling you get when you stumble on a house that's been abandoned too long, but worse. The surrounding air hummed, thick with it, a low vibration that carried a kind of malice that made her stomach twist.

Alex grunted, their jaw clenched as they braced against whatever it was. But the pressure was too much. It pushed back hard, like a wave of ice crashing against them, and Nora didn't have time to register the look of strain on Alex's face before they were both knocked off their feet.

They hit the floor together, the impact forcing the breath from their lungs as the cold bit into their skin like sharp, invisible teeth. The presence pressed down on them, heavy and suffocating, and for a split second, Nora wondered if this was what it felt like to drown—airless, help-less, pinned beneath something far too big to fight.

Ashlyn didn't move. Her hands trembled, but her feet were rooted to the floor, her eyes squeezed shut like she was listening to something distant, something awful. A spike of fear twisted in Nora's gut. This wasn't the confident ghost-hunter from the TV shows—the one who made banishing spirits look as easy as making toast. This was different. Ashlyn looked... vulnerable. Like she was balancing on a knife's edge.

Nora's breath caught in her throat. She didn't want to watch, but she couldn't look away. Ashlyn swayed, like she might topple over at any second, but then—just as Nora thought about calling out—Ashlyn's shoulders squared. There was a subtle shift, the kind you feel in the air right before a storm breaks. Her arms lifted, fingers curling to-ward the unseen force like she was reaching for something fragile and dangerous at the same time.

Nora's skin prickled, a cold sweat running down her spine. *What was she doing?* Every instinct screamed at her to grab Ashlyn, to yank her back from whatever invisible thing she was challenging. But something in the back of her mind, the part that still whispered that Ashlyn knew what she was doing, kept her rooted in place.

Still, Nora couldn't shake the feeling that they were teetering on something that, if they weren't careful, would tip them all into the abyss.

The room buckled under the strain, the walls groaning as if they might collapse, the cold so sharp it stung with every breath. Then, with a sudden crack, Ashlyn fought back. Air shimmering, and warmth rippling faintly from her hands.

The lights flickered once more, but this time they held steady. Shadows hesitated, slowly withdrawing as if tugged by an unseen force. Ashlyn exhaled, her breath misting in the air, her eyes still closed. Though pale, her expression remained resolute. Her hands, now firm, pushed the presence back, inch by inch.

The room loosened its grip, the tight, suffocating weight lifting as the shadows slunk back into the corners. The cold ebbed away, leaving only a faint, lingering chill—a ghost of what had just pressed in around them.

Ashlyn lowered her arms, her breath still unsteady but controlled, like someone who had just weathered a storm. The tension in the air snapped, like a bowstring finally released after being drawn too tight for too long.

"It's probably time to be done for the night," she said, voice soft and worn. "I've calmed him for now, but I don't want to risk it again."

She turned to Alex, brow furrowed. "Are you going to get in trouble for the light?"

"Nah, it'll be fine. I'll report it," Alex replied with a shrug. "The theater's insured through the teeth, and Martin knows how careful I am."

Ashlyn nodded, satisfied. "Good."

There was a beat of silence, thick and uneasy, before Alex broke it with a suggestion. "We should get a drink—calm the nerves."

Ashlyn gave a tight smile. "I need to get back to my hotel," she said, glancing between Nora and Alex. "But call me once the spirits settle. I'd like to see if I can reach Zeke."

"Deal," Alex said, then turned to Nora, eyebrows raised. "How about you? Drinks?"

Nora's face warmed. Was this... like a date? She tried to keep her cool, but the blush creeping up her neck betrayed her. She nodded, feeling her heart stumble over itself. "Yeah, okay."

Ashlyn waited as Alex powered down the lights and locked up the theater. When they finally stepped through the heavy double doors at the front, she handed the letters back to Nora. "Keep these. They're tied to both Helen and Zeke. If we try to reach out to them again, they'll help. But first, we need to calm Pritchard."

Nora took the tin and tucked it into her backpack with a nod.

"Want us to walk you to your car?" Alex offered, glancing at Ashlyn.

"I'm good," she replied, turning down the road. "I'm this way."

"Thank you," Alex called after her, their voice softer now. "Seriously. This means more than you know."

Ashlyn just smiled and waved before disappearing into the evening.

Alex turned back to Nora, an easy grin playing at the corners of their mouth. "There's a great spot around the corner where we go after shows. Want to check it out?"

"Sounds perfect," Nora said, a warmth rising in her body.

They led her down Tremont to a quirky little pub called The Crossroads. It was a strange mishmash of Irish pub vibes, theater memorabilia, and a dash of new-age decor thrown in for good measure. The whole place felt like it couldn't quite decide on an identity—and that made Nora love it all the more.

They slid into a booth and ordered a couple of beers, along with a plate of fries to share.

"You okay?" Alex asked, studying Nora's face.

"I will be," she said, exhaling. "Just trying to balance my relief that Zeke didn't do it with the fear of what comes next."

"Yes!" Alex agreed, their voice filled with conviction. "I didn't realize how important it was to know he was innocent until it was clear."

"Do you think there's any way to prove it?" Nora asked, her fingers tracing the rim of her glass.

Alex paused, their expression growing thoughtful. "I'm pretty sure he didn't get a fair trial... and it was so long ago. It might be easier to prove Pritchard's guilt."

"Yes!" Nora leaned forward. "It's not like the family's hard to track down. Anthony Pritchard is a big politician, and when I was doing research, I confirmed it's the same family line."

"Think you could get a meeting? Maybe they have something useful?"

Nora hesitated "I could try... but honestly, it feels like a long shot. I doubt a rich political family's going to want to admit their ancestor was a murderer."

"It's worth a try," Alex said with a lopsided grin. "Worst they can do is say no. And in the meantime, we can look into getting Zeke a posthumous pardon."

"I love that idea."

The conversation drifted into easier territory, the heavy tension easing away. Alex shared stories about their father and growing up in the city, while Nora talked about her childhood in New Hampshire, her early obsession with dance, and the feeling of freedom it gave her. The more they talked, the more the surrounding world faded into the background—just two people in a strange little corner of the world, sharing pieces of their lives over cold beers and hot fries. The air between them softened, and it felt like the rest of the world had fallen away.

Nora glanced at her watch and gasped. "Oh no! We need to go or you'll miss the last train!"

Alex's face fell, a flicker of disappointment. "I didn't realize it was so late."

Nora's heart tugged—she didn't want the night to end, either. The warmth of the pub felt like a bubble that had held them apart from the world, safe from everything waiting outside. Tomorrow, the bubble would burst, bringing back the stress of pulling off Roxie Hart, with opening night looming like a storm on the horizon.

Outside, the air was crisp, the kind that hinted at coming autumn and made you pull your jacket just a little tighter. As they walked, Alex's fingers brushed against Nora's, hesitant at first, then curling around her hand. The simple gesture sent a warmth through her, and she squeezed back, feeling a spark she wasn't ready to let go of.

When they reached the station, the looming sense of goodbye hung between them. Alex stopped, glancing down at their joined hands, then back at Nora, as if weighing a decision. They leaned in, brushing their lips gently against hers—a soft, tentative kiss.

"I really like you," Alex whispered.

CHAPTER EIGHT

In the Spotlight

When Nora arrived back at her apartment, she hovered somewhere between cloud nine and her own personal hell. Her emotions were doing a chaotic little dance, pirouetting from panic to euphoria, and occasionally taking a spin through simmering rage. She was falling for Alex. Hard. The falling where you thought, *This is fine. Everything is fine,* as you plummeted toward the ground with no parachute in sight.

Her debut in *Chicago* was looming on the horizon, a monstrous thing, full of bright lights and the potential for utter disaster. What if she flopped? What if the entire show flopped *because* of her? That was the stuff of nightmares.

Then, there was the anger—a slow, building fury at the world for ripping Helen and Zeke apart. She could almost hear the injustice humming in the back of her mind, a low, angry buzz that refused to be quieted.

She needed a distraction. Something other than her terrifying emotions and the ghosts of the past that had taken up residence in her head.

Nora opened her laptop and typed "Senator Pritchard" into the search bar. The senator's website appeared with the all-too-friendly face of a politician who wanted your vote, your donation, and—your patience with his slow website.

There it was: a contact form. Right there, waiting for her to write a letter to a man whose ancestor may or may not have been complicit in the murder of someone she'd grown far too invested in.

What exactly does one say in a letter like that? She thought, her fingers hovering over the keyboard. *Dear Senator, I'm trying to prove your great-great-grandfather was a murderer. Any help would be appreciated!*

No, that would not work.

She sighed, steeled herself, and typed.

Dear Senator Pritchard,

I hope this message finds you well. I am conducting re-search on my family history and have come across a connection to your ancestor, Edward Pritchard. As part of my study, I am hoping to find more detailed information regarding Mr. Pritchard's time in Boston, particularly any records or personal documents he may have left behind.

If you or your office have any archival materials or recommendations on where I might look for additional resources, I would greatly appreciate your guidance.

Thank you in advance for your time.

Sincerely,

Nora Sinclair

Nora sat back, feeling satisfied. It wasn't a perfect plan, but it was a start. And sometimes, in the middle of all this emotional chaos, a start was all she could hope for.

***

Nora woke the next morning with a knot in her stomach the size of a grapefruit. Dress rehearsal was tonight. *Dress Rehearsal.* All the work, all the stammering line readings, all the embarrassing false starts—it all came down to this. Martin had been patient so far, but if tonight didn't go well, she didn't know what he'd do. She wasn't sure what she would do either, except perhaps melt into a puddle of shame.

Unlikely though it was, Nora reached for her laptop. The senator wouldn't have replied—not so quickly, not after the vague little form letter she'd received from the website submission. Still, she found herself clicking into her email with that small, irrational hope gnawing at her gut.

And there it was.

From the office of Senator Pritchard.

Her heart leapt and dropped a strange little plummet of excitement and dread. With shaky fingers, she opened the email.

Dear Miss Sinclair,

Thank you for your recent correspondence. Senator Pritchard acknowledges your inquiry regarding shared ancestry and appreciates your interest. Unfortunately, after a thorough review of our records, we have found no relevant personal documents.

We regret to inform you that we are unable to assist with your request at this time. We extend our best wishes for your research and endeavors moving forward.

Sincerely,

The Office of Senator Pritchard

P.S. We hope to have your support this November!

Nora's lips pressed into a tight, thin line, the words blurring as her frustration bubbled up. The whole thing was as polite and empty as the politician himself—shiny on the surface but hollow underneath. There was no way they'd even bothered to look, not in the short time since she'd sent her inquiry.

She let out a long breath through her nose, willing herself not to scream into the laptop screen. What had she expected? A senator to hand over family secrets because she'd sent a nice email? A box of old letters and records tied up with a neat little bow?

It was clear now. She and Alex were on their own. She slammed the laptop shut, trying to ignore the fact that her hands were shaking. The senator's email had at least distracted her from the looming rehearsal for a few minutes, though the dread of it returned in full force now, slithering back into her thoughts like a vengeful snake.

Still, that cold brush-off stuck in her mind, swirling around with the rest of her worries. "Best wishes," they'd said. As if she were just another voter, they hoped to pacify before election day.

She pushed her laptop away with more force than necessary. The day was only just starting, and she was already wrapped in gloom.

***

The last week of rehearsals had passed in a blur. Helen and Zeke were pushed to the back burner. Each day, the cast sharpened their timing, refined their choreography, and smoothed over the rough edges. But for Nora, the pressure mounted in a way she hadn't expected. She had pushed through her self-doubt before, but this was something else.

Martin had pushed them hard. "Roxie's lines need to *snap*, Nora!" he called from the front row. "I need fire, I need attitude, I need you to *own* it."

Nora nodded, doing her best to channel the confident swagger of Roxie Hart, but she wasn't owning it. She was still pretending. But in the back of her mind, the doubts kept creeping in: *Am I good enough? What if I ruin this? What if everyone sees through me?*

The last notes of "All That Jazz," rang out, and Martin clapped his hands. "That's a wrap for today. You've got a day to breathe before dress rehearsal."

Nora forced a smile as the cast trickled out, their voices fading like the last echoes of a song. She lingered, letting the empty theater press in around her. The energy that had filled the space moments ago evaporated, leaving only a heavy, hollow quiet. The walls seemed to creep closer, swallowing every scrap of laughter and conversation. Her stomach churned, sharp and heavy, like she'd swallowed a fistful of gravel.

"Nora, can I see you?" Martin's voice cut through the quiet, pulling her attention. He stood waiting, arms folded across his chest like he was bracing for something unpleasant.

She swallowed hard and made her way toward him, already feeling the sting of impending disappointment. Maybe it was the way he looked at her—eyes narrowed, lips pressed together in a thin line. Not good.

"Sweetheart, you are too nice," he said, his tone so matter-of-fact it felt like a slap.

Nora blinked, surprised by the bluntness. She opened her mouth, but no words came. Too nice? She'd been told that before—by strangers, by friends, by an ex who once said it like it was an apology. But hearing it from Martin, someone who was supposed to believe in her, hit different.

"And I can tell," he added, his lips still tight, as if he'd been holding back the critique for a while.

"There are worse things to be," Nora said, forcing a crooked smile that even she didn't believe. It was an olive branch, a flimsy one, expecting some reassurance or at least a little sympathy. A laugh, maybe.

But Martin's expression didn't budge. "I just don't believe it." He shook his head, his disappointment hanging between them. "Your performance is hollow. Roxie is not nice, Nora. She's calculating, and—" He waved a hand, searching for the right word. "She's selfish. There's nothing about her that says 'nice.'"

He trailed off, and the silence felt like it was settling into her bones.

Nora's throat tightened. She could feel the tears pricking at the back of her eyes, but she blinked them away. Where was the Martin who had believed in her? The one who had picked her, who had seen something in her that even she couldn't see? She wanted to ask him, wanted to grab onto that moment and shake it until it came back.

Instead, she nodded, trying to swallow the lump in her throat, even though it felt like it might choke her.

Martin sighed, the sound heavy with exhaustion, or maybe frustration. "Look," he said, rubbing the back of his neck like the conversation had worn him out. "You've got potential, Nora. But Roxie? I need more from you. More grit. More... something. Because right now, I just don't buy it."

She nodded again, though every word felt like another nail in the coffin of her confidence. "I can do better," she said, the words leaving her mouth before she even realized she was saying them. It was a promise she wasn't sure she could keep.

He gave her a long, unreadable look, then sighed again, his gaze drifting somewhere over her shoulder. "I've got a lot to think about."

That didn't sound good. Nora's stomach churned, and she felt like she might be sick this time.

Martin turned away, already moving toward the wings. "Lexi!" he called out, his voice bouncing off the theater walls. The name echoed in the hollow space, leaving Nora standing alone as his words settled in.

And just like that, he disappeared, running after her understudy.

At that moment, something inside her snapped. A cold, sharp crack, like ice breaking underfoot. He didn't believe in her. Of course he didn't. No one ever did. And no one ever would, would they? She could feel it—the years of frustration, of trying to prove herself, of being just *not enough*—all of it boiling up, ready to explode.

If she was going to do anything, it would have to be on her own.

"Not tall enough, my ass," she muttered under her breath, the words sharp, like they'd been burning inside her for far too long. "Not good enough? Not Roxie enough? What a joke." Her hands trembled, and she shoved them into her pockets, her breath coming fast and shallow.

She swayed for a moment, unsteady, as if every rejection she'd ever felt was finally pressing down on her. The auditions, the cutthroat competition, the constant reminder that she was never *quite* right. Just a little off, a little less than what everyone else wanted. But she would not crumble. Not today.

The theater felt suffocating, the walls too close, the air too thick. Her heart pounded, but it wasn't from nerves. It was anger—hot, consuming, and, for the first time in a long time, productive. If they didn't believe in her, then screw them. She'd prove them wrong. She'd show them all.

Alex's voice called her name in the distance, soft and filled with concern. Nora didn't care. Sympathy wasn't what she wanted, nor did she need anyone's coddling or reassurance. What she needed was action—and she needed it now.

Without a second glance, she stormed toward the door, her footsteps heavy and purposeful, stomping out every shred of self-doubt that had been planted in her. She shoved the door open with more force than necessary, the cool evening air hitting her like a slap to the face, but it barely registered. Her mind was already racing, already deciding what to do next.

Nora hardly registered getting on the Blue Line. The train clattered along, its noise blending into the steady hum of her thoughts, all sharp edges and rising fury. Before she even realized it, she was standing at the front door of Senator Pritchard's house, her heart pounding more from anger than anything else. How had she ended up here? The details were fuzzy, but the goal was clear. She was done waiting for people to believe in her. If she was going to make a difference, if she was going to exonerate Zeke, she'd have to take matters into her own hands.

The house loomed in front of her, all rich, dark stone and ironwork, like it had been plucked straight from a Gothic novel. The tall windows reflected the night, giving it an air of cold indifference. She approached and knocked, her knuckles smarting from the force of it. The door creaked open with the heavy, old-world sound that made her think of ancient castles and the sort of places that had hidden dungeons.

An older man answered—tall, stiff, and dressed in black. A butler. She almost laughed, a harsh little noise stuck in the back of her throat. Did rich people *actually* still have butlers? Of course, Senator Pritchard would. It suited the level of pompous she'd imagined.

"I'm looking for Senator Pritchard," she said, her tone hard enough to cut glass. Her head buzzed with the fury still thrumming beneath her skin. "My name is Roxane Hartman, and I have an appointment."

The butler's face shifted as he looked her up and down, eyes scanning her with the disapproving scrutiny that made her skin itch. He was judging her. Of course he was. She didn't belong in a place like this. To him, she was some nobody off the street.

"I'm sorry," he said after a pause, his voice smooth and polite in the most condescending way possible. "There are no appointments on the schedule."

Nora felt her patience fray, like a thread being pulled too tight. "Check again," she snapped, stepping halfway into the doorway before he could even react.

His eyes widened just a fraction, but it was enough. He wasn't expecting a confrontation—not from her. The rush of power that followed surprised her. Maybe she was more like Roxie Hart than she thought.

The butler hesitated, weighing his options. After a tense moment, he dipped his head and disappeared around the corner, presumably to check the schedule or to tell Pritchard there was a crazy woman at the door. Either way, he was gone.

Perfect.

Without a second thought, Nora slipped inside. The entryway was grand, of course—tall ceilings, intricate molding, polished floors that gleamed under the dim light of a chandelier that looked like it belonged in a ballroom. She glanced around, her gaze falling on a door to her left that led to what looked like a library. The bookshelves were tall and stuffed with volumes that hadn't been touched in years. Rich people's bookshelves were never for reading, were they?

But if she was going to find anything useful—anything that could exonerate Zeke—it would be somewhere in that office. Her anger fueled her as she crossed the room, her footsteps too loud in the quiet space, but she didn't care. She scanned the shelves, her hands itching to pull books down, to tear the place apart if she had to.

But then... the heat cooled. The farther she got into the room, the more the anger drained away, like water slipping through her fingers. What had she been thinking? She wasn't some mastermind spy. She was Nora Sinclair, a dancer who got tongue-tied on stage and had never even *sneaked* into a movie without paying, much less a senator's house.

Her hand paused over the spine of an old leather-bound book, something important-looking and weathered. Without thinking, she pulled it from the shelf and cracked it open, expecting secret codes or some dusty old ledger. Instead, she stared at the title page of a first edition of Robert Frost's poems.

The words "First edition" caught her eye. Wow. Her fingers lightly traced the pages, lingering over the poetry she adored. For a moment, she stood still, the scent of old paper filling the air. Her heart quieted, and the earlier storm of anger gave way to a slow, creeping sadness.

With a sigh, she closed the book and slid it back onto the shelf. The world was right; she really was too nice.

A soft cough sounded behind her, and her stomach plummeted. She turned, half-expecting to see the butler ready to throw her out or maybe even call the police. Instead, there he was, standing just behind her. His face was unreadable, though his eyes flickered with something—surprise, maybe. Amusement?

"Miss Hartman," the butler said, his voice low and calm, as if the situation wasn't weird at all. Maybe this *was* just what happened in rich people's houses all the time. He didn't look shocked or angry, just inconvenienced, like someone who had found a stray cat in the parlor. "I have the police on hold. You should leave."

Nora's face went hot, her blush so fierce it felt like her skin might catch fire. She stammered, "Ss-sorry," the words barely escaping her throat, and before she could think of anything else, she turned and bolted. Her boots echoed on the polished floors as she fled, every step screaming failure, failure, failure.

She yanked the door open and stumbled out into the night, the heavy wooden door closing with a solid thud behind her. The cool air hit her like a shock, but she didn't stop. She crossed the street, not noticing the world around her—cars, the faint hum of city life—until she found herself at a pedestrian walkway lined with trees and benches.

There, beneath the canopy of branches and surrounded by the muffled quiet of the city park, she collapsed onto a bench. Her hands flew to her face, and she buried her head in them, humiliation burning through her. She'd done it this time. Broken into a senator's house, stammered like an idiot in front of an actual butler, and then nearly gotten the cops called on her. All in the name of some half-baked plan to find evidence. What was she even thinking?

She wasn't thinking. That was the problem.

Nora let out a shaky breath and wiped her eyes, which had stung with the threat of tears. What now? Who was she supposed to call? It wasn't like she had a lot of options. Her boss? Linda would be kind, of course, but she wouldn't understand. Linda would pat her on the head and tell her to take a hot bath and meditate on her chakras or something. Martin? Yeah, right. Martin already thought she was a disaster.

With a sigh, she pulled out her phone and stared at the screen, her thumb hovering over the contacts list. After a long pause, she dialed Alex. It took less than a minute for them to answer. And within twenty, Alex was sitting next to her on the bench, their presence a warm and comforting.

They said nothing at first, just sat there, the park's streetlights casting soft shadows on the grass. Alex was good at that—knowing when to speak and when to just... be.

Finally, after a long stretch of silence, Alex glanced at her. "What were you thinking?" they asked, their tone gentle but not without a hint of you did this, didn't-you?

Nora let out a dry laugh. "That's the thing," she said, running a hand through her tangled hair. "I wasn't thinking. I just..." she trailed off, feeling her throat tighten. How could she explain it? The frustration, the endless feeling of not being good enough, the desperate need to do *something* right for once.

Alex didn't push, just slid an arm around her shoulders, and Nora leaned into them. She rested her head against Alex's shoulder and closed her eyes, willing the world to stop spinning for just a minute.

"I just wanted to do something right," she whispered. "I wanted to prove Zeke innocent. I thought—if I could just find something, anything—it would make all this worth it. Like I could actually... matter."

Alex's arm tightened around her, their hand giving her shoulder a reassuring squeeze. "Nora," they said, "you're enough

***

The day of the dress rehearsal arrived far too soon for Nora's liking. The Majestic Theatre buzzed with the familiar, chaotic energy of last-minute preparations—crew members shouting instructions, props being shuffled into place, and the constant hum of nervous excitement. But as Nora stood backstage in her Roxie costume, all that movement felt distant, like a storm rolling in from miles away.

Her heart pounded. At first, it was just a flutter, something small and ignorable. But then it grew, swelling into a full-on stampede. Her breaths came shallow, sharp. Too sharp. Her hands trembled at her sides, the sensation alien, like they weren't even hers. Was this a heart attack? Oh god, she was too young to die!

What's happening?

Nora leaned back against the wall, trying to steady herself, but it only made things worse. The harder she tried to control it, the more it spiraled out of her reach. Her vision blurred, and the familiar sights of the theater—the velvet curtains, the wooden boards—wobbled and stretched like something out of a bad dream. She could hear her own heartbeat pounding in her ears, drowning out everything else.

She gasped for air, but no matter how much she pulled in, it wasn't enough.

I can't breathe. Oh god. What's wrong with me?

Panic crashed over her like a wave, stealing the breath from her lungs and the ground from under her feet. The dread that had been building all week pulled her down, sinking her deeper and deeper. She wasn't Roxie; she was just Nora—the too-nice, too-small girl who didn't belong here.

Roxie Hart... The thought of her character clawed its way into her mind. Roxie, the conniving, manipulative woman who shoots her lover and walks away scot-free, acquitted and adored. How was it that someone like Roxie—a murderer—could charm her way out of a death sentence while someone like Zeke, who didn't hurt anyone, was convicted and executed for murder? It wasn't fair. None of it was.

Her pulse raced even faster as her thoughts spiraled. Roxie gets to walk free. But Zeke... Zeke never stood a chance. He'd been convicted, his life taken, for a crime Nora was sure he didn't commit. How many Roxies had the world let off the hook? How many real-life Roxies used charm, luck, and privilege to escape the consequences of their actions, while innocent people like Zeke were punished?

The realization hit her like a train, and the floor didn't feel real anymore. *Roxie's fictional, she's fictional,* she chanted to herself. But it didn't stop the world from spinning. There were too many Roxies out there—too much injustice. And Zeke? Zeke was real. He never got to plead his case.

Her breath stuttered. Her lungs seemed to shrink, folding in on themselves like someone was squeezing them with both hands. She blinked, but her vision was blurry, as though the world had been smeared with fog. Roxie's swagger felt like a sick joke now, something she could never hold on to. How was she supposed to play a woman everyone loved, when Zeke's story—his truth—was all wrong?

"Nora?"

Martin's voice snapped through the haze like a twig breaking underfoot, harsh and loud. Too loud. She couldn't stand it. His words grated against her thoughts, dragging her back to the present, but not in the way she needed. *I can't do this.* He stood a few feet away, brows furrowed in that familiar "what now?" look.

"You look... pale," he said, eyeing her like a ticking bomb. "Are you alright?"

She tried to answer, but her throat was dry, and her tongue felt like lead. She opened her mouth, but all that came out was a ragged, shallow breath. *This isn't happening. Please, not now.*

Her pulse hammered—roaring in her ears like the ocean was crashing down on her. Everything else was fading, blurring, *vanishing.* The world was spinning too fast, and she wasn't part of it anymore.

"Lexi!" Martin barked, a sound like nails on glass. The words crashed into her like a punch, knocking the breath out of her again.

Lexi appeared, looking every bit the Roxie Nora couldn't be—polished, smug, *ready.* Nora's stomach twisted. She was slipping. She was losing everything, and she couldn't even speak to stop it.

Her chest was so tight now, every breath scraping like broken glass, and just when she thought she might crumble into pieces on the floor, a hand touched her shoulder. It was gentle but firm, like an anchor yanking her out of the storm. She flinched at the contact but didn't pull away.

"Nora, hey." Alex's voice was soft but solid, cutting through the noise. "Look at me."

She blinked, struggling to focus on their face through the haze. Their presence felt... real. Something to cling to.

"Breathe with me, okay? In through the nose, out through the mouth."

Her breath hitched again, shallow and painful. "I don't—" she rasped, her voice strangled. "I don't know what's happening." She wasn't sure she could breathe at all anymore. She wasn't sure of anything except that she was falling apart, right there in front of everyone.

Alex's hand stayed on her shoulder, grounding her. "You're having a panic attack," they said, matter-of-fact, like it was something as normal as rain.

A panic attack. That's what this was? But she didn't have panic attacks. Not like this. She tried to explain, to say something, but her throat was tight, and the words didn't come.

Alex inhaled, showing her, slow and steady. "In through the nose. Hold it. Now out through the mouth."

Nora tried to copy them, but her lungs felt like they were stuck in a vise. Still, she followed, even though each breath felt too thin, too shallow. But Alex kept going, guiding her.

"That's it," they murmured, and somehow, their voice was calming—like a rhythm she could cling to. "Just keep going. You're doing fine."

Gradually, the world came back into focus. The tightness eased just a fraction, enough that she could feel the floor beneath her feet again, real. She wasn't floating away anymore.

She squeezed her eyes shut, then opened them, gasping. "I'm... I'm sorry," she whispered, her voice trembling. "I don't know what—"

"You don't have to apologize," Alex said, and their voice was so gentle it made her want to cry all over again. "It happens. But you're okay. You're going to be okay."

Martin was still there, arms crossed and looking like he wanted to say something, but Alex raised their hand, keeping him back. They turned back to Nora.

"You've been rehearsing for weeks," they said, meeting her eyes. "You know this, Nora. Your body knows what to do. Let it take over."

Nora's breathing was still shaky, and her legs were like jelly, but she wasn't drowning anymore, and the fog was lifting. "I don't know if I can do this," she admitted.

Alex stood and offered her their hand. "You've got this. You've earned this role. The only thing standing in your way is the fear. You're stronger than that."

The words hit her like a challenge, echoing inside her. *Fear.* Maybe that's what this all was, at the heart of it. Fear. And hadn't Roxie thrived on fear? Turned it into power?

She took a breath, still shaky, still unsure, but deeper this time. Steadier. Hesitantly, she reached out and took Alex's hand, pulling herself to her feet.

"Lexi, stay ready," Martin called, still hovering, but Nora barely heard him now. He wasn't the point. The stage was.

Her legs wobbled as she stood, but she stayed upright. Alex's hand, warm and steady, gave her balance.

"One breath at a time," they reminded her, squeezing her hand before letting go. "You've got this. I'll be right here in the wings."

Nora took another breath, shaky but real, and the spark of determination inside her flared just enough to feel possible. She wasn't Roxie yet, but maybe, maybe she could be.

She stepped into the spotlight.

CHAPTER NINE

Curtain Call

Backstage was its usual charming disaster. People were running around, set pieces were being wrestled into place, and someone was muttering about a missing prop. The doors were opening soon, but no one looked like they believed that. It was the good chaos—the kind that usually meant things were going to turn out fine, even if it didn't look that way right now.

Nora stood with the others onstage, waiting. Martin called over the crew, and Alex slipped in beside her, giving her hand a quick, reassuring squeeze. She squeezed back, grateful for the moment of calm in all the noise. But even in the buzz of pre-show excitement, there was something else. The faint sensation that someone—or something—was watching. She felt it like a soft touch on the back of her neck; the hairs rising.

She scanned the wings and the back of the theater, half-expecting to glimpse someone. Was it just nerves? She thought about what Ashlyn had said. Receptive. Empathic. The word had settled in her mind like a key turning in a lock she hadn't known was there. It had given her something to hold on to, an explanation for why she felt so connected to Helen, why she couldn't shake the story of Zeke's conviction.

Now, standing under the dim backstage lights, it felt real. She imagined Zeke in the back row, watching from the shadows, his eyes fixed on her, waiting.

Martin cleared his throat, the way he always did before one of his little speeches. "Okay, everyone—my job's done. Now it's all on you. I trust you to do your jobs, own the stage, and shine. Break a leg!"

As Martin spoke, Nora half-listened, her thoughts drifting. Somewhere in the back of her mind, she could almost hear Helen's voice—soft, steady, and ready to step into the spotlight. Did Helen ever feel like this? That strange cocktail of excitement and dread, like her heart, was trying to dance and hide at the same time? Maybe she had, just before stepping on stage, with a crowd waiting and everything on the line. Or maybe Helen had been braver, stronger—someone who didn't unravel when the pressure hit.

Martin started for the house, then paused just long enough to lean in close to Nora. "You've got this, girl. Knock 'em dead."

The crew scattered to their places, and Nora felt it—the familiar tingle of adrenaline. But this time, it wasn't panic. This was the good kind, the kind that used to hit her right before a dance performance. Something clicked into place, like sliding on an old, comfortable pair of shoes. She could do this. It did not differ from letting her body take over and do what it knew how to do.

Everyone was set. The audience hushed. Somewhere, a child squealed, and Nora smiled. *You're gonna love this one, Ollie.* Her breath steadied, her heart slowing into a familiar rhythm.

One last glance toward the wings, and she could have sworn she saw a figure there—a fleeting, ghostly shadow, the outline of a woman, watching her.

The lights dimmed, the curtain rose, and Nora stepped into the spotlight.

**

The next three weeks passed in a blur of sequins, stage lights, and breathless applause. It was an odd sensation—so much work, so many long rehearsals, all for the briefest whirlwind of performances. But every minute had been worth it. Nora felt like she was eating, sleeping, and breathing Roxie Hart. (And there had been a lot of sleeping, too. Even Roxie needed her beauty rest.)

The hunt for Zeke's story, the mystery she and Alex had become so wrapped up in, had been shoved to the back burner. She didn't have time to think about anything other than stage cues and costume changes. But on that final night, as the audience's applause faded, and they took their last bows, Zeke and Helen crept back into her thoughts, as persistent as ever.

As the cast and crew packed up and started trickling out of the theater, Nora hung around, loitering like a shadow in the corner. She wasn't quite ready to leave the stage just yet.

Alex was still there, of course. They were in their element, directing the crew to dismantle the set and making sure the theater was shut down, their voice carrying over the sound of footsteps and packing crates.

"Hey!" they called when they finally noticed Nora lurking. "Martin throws a mad post-production party—you should be there. You earned it."

"Are you going?" Nora asked.

"Yeah, but I've got to finish up here first."

"I'll wait," Nora smiled. "We can head over together."

Alex smiled back. "May as well put you to work, then." They nodded toward the dust mop leaning in the corner. "Want to get the stage?"

"Of course!" Nora grinned.

She grabbed the mop and pushed it across the stage, sweeping up bits of glitter, confetti, and the odd prop piece. As she swung back toward Alex, she said, "I think I saw Zeke tonight, you know…"

That got Alex's attention. They stopped mid-task, looking over at her. "He was watching from the back of the house," she continued, making another pass with the mop. "He seemed sad."

Another pass. "And Helen was with me, too."

When Nora finished sweeping, Alex joined her at center stage. "We need to finish what we started, don't we?"

Nora nodded. The performances had been amazing, but this felt just as important.

"I think I have an idea…" Alex said.

Nora's curiosity flared. "What is it?" she asked.

"Let me smooth it out first, okay? Don't want to jump the gun."

"Alright, but don't leave me in the dark too long!"

As they spoke, Nora's gaze drifted toward the balcony, where she saw a lone figure—a man—sitting in the shadows at the back. He wasn't part of the crew. She knew, without a doubt, who he was. Zeke. Watching, waiting.

She nudged Alex, and when they followed her gaze, they gave a small, solemn nod. No one else noticed, but Nora didn't need anyone else to see. She knew.

Then, without another word, she and Alex headed off-stage and through the backstage hallway, leaving behind the ghostly image of Helen, standing near the wings, still watching the empty theater with eyes full of longing.

"We'll fix this," Nora whispered as the door clicked shut behind them.

***

The next night, Nora and Alex were back at the theater, this time with Ashlyn Alden joining them. The party had been a blast. While Nora felt closest to Martin and Alex, there was still a sense of camaraderie with the rest of the cast—a shared pride in what they'd accomplished. No matter their backgrounds, they had all been on the same team. Nora had too much to drink, though, and she'd spent the entire day sleeping it off. Luckily, she lived within walking distance.

"Before we try to contact Zeke," Ashlyn said as they entered the lobby, "we need to make sure Pritchard isn't a threat."

"How do we do that?" Alex asked.

"By confining him to his own space." Ashlyn grinned. "From what we've uncovered, he was a man of immense pride. He's angry because he doesn't want to be blamed for Helen's death. But he killed her in a fit of rage—like a toddler smashing another kid's toy because he couldn't play with it."

Ashlyn wandered over to the giant painting of Edward Pritchard hanging in the lobby. "We need to show him that he's still revered, and then we'll build a barrier to keep him confined to this space."

"Is it too much to ask to just banish him?" Nora asked, frowning.

Ashlyn smiled. "You can only banish spirits who agree to leave, and I don't think we'll be convincing Pritchard of that. But we can make him feel adored, secure in his pride."

"So, trick him?" Alex asked.

Ashlyn held a finger to her lips. "Careful, he could be listening. Based on our previous sessions here, I've never detected a powerful presence in the foyer. It's a suitable space. Let's get started."

The air in the theater lobby was thick enough to chew. Nora, Alex, and Ashlyn stood in a loose triangle near the towering portrait of Edward Pritchard. Even from within the frame, his eyes seemed to follow them.

Ashlyn closed her eyes, exhaling, like she was listening for something just out of reach. Her hands hovered at her sides, fingers twitching once or twice, before she stilled.

"We need to make him feel at home," Ashlyn said. "Pritchard was all about pride. We can use that. Pride anchors spirits like him—it keeps them from flying off in a rage or, you know, haunting toilets."

Alex raised an eyebrow. "Toilets?"

"Some have a flair for drama," Ashlyn replied, deadpan. "We don't want him haunting the ladies' room. Trust me."

She turned and made her way toward Pritchard's portrait, resting her hands on the frame. "This is where he will feel the strongest connection—the foyer, the entrance to his domain. It's like... a king at the gates of his castle. He needs to feel respected."

Alex looked skeptical, but kept quiet. Nora shifted, her gaze darting between Ashlyn and the portrait, as though expecting the ghost to pop out at any second.

Ashlyn knelt and pulled a small bag of herbs and salt from her coat pocket. With a practiced flick of her wrist, she started sprinkling the mixture in a neat circle around the base of the portrait. "We're building him a little sanctuary," she explained, muttering something that might have been in Latin—or possibly just gibber-ish. Nora wasn't sure.

"What's the salt for?" Nora asked, her voice soft.

"To create a boundary," Ashlyn said, looking up. "This isn't about banishing him. You can't banish someone un-less they want to go and let's face it—Pritchard's not the 'willing to be exiled' type. But we can make this space feel important to him, a place where he'll want to stay."

Alex crossed their arms, half amused, half concerned.

Ashlyn gave a faint smile. "We're giving him what he thinks he deserves. To him, this will feel like an offer-ing." She finished the circle and stood up, brushing her hands off. "He's getting a fancy little velvet rope to keep him happy. And inside that rope, he'll feel like the king of the world."

Alex glanced at the portrait. "Not sure he needs any help with that."

Once the circle was complete, Ashlyn lit a small candle and placed it in front of the painting. The flame flick-ered and danced, casting odd, jittery shadows that made Pritchard's already unnerving face seem to glower even harder.

Ashlyn took another deep breath, holding her palms up toward the portrait. "Edward Pritchard," she called, her voice as smooth as silk, "we invite you into this space. This is your domain. You are honored here, remembered here."

Nora felt the temperature drop. Not dramatically, but enough that the hair on her arms stood up. The candle flame wavered, shrinking for a moment before flaring brighter. She exchanged a glance with Alex, whose wide eyes suggested they weren't as comfortable with this as they were trying to seem.

"He's here," Ashlyn said, as if she were commenting on the weather. She opened her eyes, now fixed on the empty space in front of the painting.

"Edward," she began, her voice taking on a gentle, coaxing tone, "we know your story. We know you don't want to be blamed for what happened to Helen. You were angry. But that anger wasn't meant to destroy her, was it? You were frustrated, not... cruel."

A shiver rolled through the room, like the theater itself had taken a breath. The candle's flame guttered again, then steadied.

"You don't need to haunt this place in anger anymore," Ashlyn continued, her tone soothing, like she was trying to coax a spooked animal out of hiding. "Your legacy is here, Edward. This foyer is your space. You are powerful here. Respected. Revered."

Nora squinted at the shadows near the painting. Had they always been so... deep? Something was there, listening, deciding.

"You belong here, Edward," Ashlyn continued. "This is where you will stay. You will not interfere with the others. You will not go beyond this boundary."

For a long moment, the room was as still as a graveyard at midnight. Nora held her breath without realizing it. Then, the heavy pressure in the air lifted, like someone had opened a window and let out a long-held sigh.

Ashlyn exhaled, the tension draining from her posture. "He's agreed. As long as we respect this space, he'll stay confined to the foyer."

"Just like that?" Alex's voice was a little higher than usual, glancing at the painting.

Ashlyn gave a small, satisfied smile. "Spirits are a lot like people. They want to feel important. And if you give them what they think they deserve, they're usually happy."

Nora felt her chest lighten. There was more work to do, more spirits to deal with, but for now, at least, Edward Pritchard was no longer a problem. They could finally focus on Zeke.

"Now," Ashlyn said, dusting her hands off, "let's go talk to someone who wants to be helped."

"I saw him on the balcony," Nora said, her voice quiet but certain, leading them toward the stairs.

They climbed the narrow staircase, each step making the air feel a little cooler, a little heavier. By the time they reached the top, Nora couldn't shake the feeling that the theater was holding its breath, waiting for something. The old balcony seats stretched out in the dim light, their worn red cushions contrasting the shadows. The whole place felt... watchful, but not in a bad way. It was eerie, sure, but there was something peaceful about it too, like the ghosts here had already settled in for the night.

Ashlyn stood at the balcony, her gaze sweeping over the rows of chairs. Nora could feel the tension in the air—the kind that prickled at your skin, like you were being watched, even if no one was there.

Ashlyn closed her eyes and inhaled. "Zeke," she called, her voice calm but firm, "we're here for you. We know you've been waiting."

Nothing happened. No sudden chill, no flicker of shadows—just the silence of an empty theater.

Alex glanced around, eyebrows raised. "So much for someone who wants to be helped."

Ashlyn sighed. "He's here," she said under her breath, eyes still closed. "He's just... reluctant." She opened her eyes, her gaze now fixed on the far corner of the balcony. "Zeke, we're here to help. We know what happened."

Still, the air was thick with silence.

Ashlyn's face tightened with concentration. "He's... upset," she said slowly. "Wary."

Alex shifted their weight, uncomfortable with the invisible conversation happening in front of them. "Can't blame him," they muttered. "But how do we get him to listen?"

Ashlyn turned, her eyes locking on Alex. "You," she said. "You're his family. That's what he needs to hear."

Alex blinked, surprised. "Uh, what?"

Ashlyn nodded toward the shadowy end of the balcony. "You're from his brother's line. He knows that."

Alex glanced at the darkness and then back to Ashlyn. "You sure he knows? Because it feels like I'm about to give a speech to the floor."

Ashlyn gave them a look, her patience running thin. "Trust me."

Alex sighed but stepped forward, clearing their throat. "Zeke," they began, "I'm Alex Turner. My family—your family—came from your brother's side. We're... connected."

For a moment, nothing happened. Then, there was a noticeable shift—a chill in the air, like a door had opened somewhere far off. Ashlyn straightened, eyes widening. "He's listening."

Nora couldn't help but shiver. She couldn't see Zeke, but she could feel something, a presence hanging back in the shadows. It wasn't menacing, just... sad. Heavy with regret.

Ashlyn's voice softened, as though speaking to someone fragile. "Zeke," she said, "Alex is your family. They've come here to help. We want to reunite you with Helen. She's been waiting for you all this time."

Nora held her breath, waiting. The shadows seemed to shift, deepen. It was as if Zeke was there, just out of sight, but not quite willing to step forward.

Ashlyn tilted her head, her expression becoming more focused, as if she were hearing something the rest of them couldn't. "He's... not ready."

Alex let out a frustrated huff. "What do you mean, he's not ready? Helen's been waiting for him. We've been working to clear his name. This is what he's been stuck here for, isn't it?"

Ashlyn winced, as if absorbing a hard truth. "He thinks he doesn't deserve it," she murmured. "He believes Helen deserves better."

Nora's chest tightened. "But he didn't kill her," she said, her voice almost pleading. "He wasn't a murderer. We can fix this."

Ashlyn nodded, eyes still distant, as if half of her mind was elsewhere, communing with the spirit. "He's not listening to that. It's not about the truth—it's about what everyone believed. He's been carrying that weight, and now..." She paused, then added, "He doesn't want her to be stuck with him."

The air around them felt thick with sorrow. Nora glanced toward the shadows where Zeke's presence hovered, feeling a pang of frustration. "But Helen's been waiting for him," she whispered. "Doesn't he know that?"

Ashlyn's lips tightened. "He knows. But he doesn't think he deserves her. Not anymore."

A deep, quiet silence fell over them, the kind that felt like the end of a conversation, whether or not they wanted it to be.

Alex sighed, running a hand through their hair. "So... what now? We just leave him?"

Ashlyn took a slow breath, lowering her hands. "Sometimes... spirits have to come to terms with things on their own time. We can't force him to move on."

Nora stared at the space where Zeke lingered, her heart heavy with disappointment. She had wanted this to work—to help him, to bring him back to Helen. But as she looked at the dark corners of the balcony, she knew there was nothing more they could do tonight.

"We'll come back," Ashlyn said, as though speaking to Zeke himself. "We're not giving up. But for now... rest."

The chill in the air lightened, the strange heaviness beginning to lift. Whatever connection Ashlyn had been holding faded, and the theater felt like just a theater again—no ghostly presence, no lingering regret. Just silence.

Ashlyn turned to Nora and Alex. "There's nothing more we can do today."

Nora gave one last glance toward the darkened balcony, feeling the unfinished business hanging in the air. Zeke wasn't ready, and that hurt more than she expected. But maybe... maybe one day, he would be.

"We'll fix this," Nora whispered, more to herself than to anyone else, as they made their way down the stairs and out into the cool night air.

The theater door clicked shut behind them, leaving the balcony—and Zeke—alone in the quiet.

The three of them headed to The Crossroads. Nora slumped into her chair, feeling defeated. "I can't get proof to exonerate him, and Zeke doesn't seem to want to act without it."

Alex gave one of their lopsided grins, the kind that usually meant they were about to drop something big. "I think I'm ready to share my idea…"

They pulled a stack of printed papers from their bag and set it on the table.

"What is it?" Nora asked, eyeing the stack.

"It's a play," Alex said, leaning back. "A tragedy. Telling Helen and Zeke's story."

Nora blinked, not sure if they were serious. "A play?"

"Yeah. We tell their actual story—everything we've learned. Zeke's version, the truth. People love tragic love stories, especially with a murder mystery twist. We get people talking, revisiting the case, and it might even reach the folks who can do something about clearing Zeke's name."

Ashlyn, who had been quiet, raised an eyebrow. "And you think a play is going to convince people that a century-old ghost story is real?"

"Why not," Alex shrugged. "You do it on T.V. shows. People believe what you make them feel. We can't get Zeke exonerated through facts alone, but if we turn his story into something that tugs at the heartstrings? That can change how people see him."

Ashlyn looked at the script. "It's not a bad idea," she admitted. "If we can't change public opinion with hard evidence, we change it with emotion. People love a good ghost story. And this one is full of heartbreak."

Nora leaned back, considering it. It was crazy. But then, everything about this situation was crazy. "So we rewrite history as a tragedy?"

"No," Alex corrected, their grin widening, "we set the record straight."

Nora felt a flicker of hope. "And we're doing this for Zeke and Helen? To clear their names?"

"For them. For the theater. And maybe, a little, for us," Alex said. "I have enough pull that I think we can get the production funded."

"I may be able to help, too," Ashlyn added.

Nora shook her head but couldn't help smiling. Leave it to Alex to turn tragedy into something hopeful. "Alright. Let's do it."

CHAPTER TEN

Finale

Alex worked tirelessly on the play, and Nora was right there by their side, day in and day out. It was a modest production, a labor of love. The cast was so small that everyone did everything—props, costumes, even painting the set. Alex, with their quiet focus, directed the production with a kind of relentless, joyful determination that left Nora breathless. And, of course, who better to play Zeke and Helen than the two of them?

History clung to them during every rehearsal, heavy and undeniable. There were moments when Nora could almost feel Helen's presence hovering in the wings, her spirit watching, waiting for her story to be told. And Zeke—well, Nora suspected Alex could feel him, too. Sometimes they'd exchange a look during rehearsal, and Alex would give her that small, secret smile as if to say, *They're still here with us, aren't they?*

It was a one-night-only performance, gifted by the theater association with a reluctant nod to Alex's persistence. One night. The entire production hinged on a single chance, like a high-wire act without a net. And yet, it was all they needed.

The moment Linda got wind of it, she plastered the city with flyers, tapping into her dance studio connections, and Martin—ever the subtle mastermind—spoke in low tones to the right people in Boston's theater scene. Word spread. Calvin Turner, Zeke's great-nephew, turned out to be the play's most devoted advocate, charming anyone who would listen with stories about Zeke and Helen, their doomed love, and the injustice of their story.

By the time the day of the performance arrived, even the cast of *Chicago*—Nora's old crew—had rallied behind them, their voices echoing through the city's coffee shops and social media channels.

Senator Pritchard, sitting in the audience, was perhaps the only question mark of the evening. Nora had spotted him as soon as he entered, moving through the seats with all the ease of someone used to controlling rooms much bigger than this one. His ancestor's portrayal was hardly flattering, and Nora's stomach twisted at the thought of what he might say afterward. She hoped, prayed, that the man had enough of a care to see the performance for what it was—a story, a reckoning. But if he didn't, well...he'd have to deal with it. The truth had been buried long enough.

And then there was Ashlyn. Oh, Ashlyn. Ever the opportunist, she had mentioned the show in one of her ghost-hunting episodes. Nora had seen the gleam in her eye when she'd said it — "Ghosts, history, romance," she'd grinned. "Who could resist?" The mention worked. That evening, a good chunk of the audience was there just as much, hoping to see one of the Majestic's infamous spirits as in the story itself. Some had come with cameras, whispering about orbs and temperature changes. *Let them hunt their ghosts,* Nora thought, as long as the message got across.

The house lights dimmed, and Nora's heart thundered, a pulsing rhythm in time with the scuff of feet settling into seats. She stood in the wings, her breath held, waiting. The air was thick with anticipation, the kind that felt like it might spark into a storm at any moment. She glanced at Alex, standing just a few feet away, their head bowed, eyes closed as if they were centering themselves. When they looked up, they gave her a small nod, calm and reassuring, the sort of gesture that said, *We're ready. We've got this.*

Nora exhaled, feeling the floor beneath her feet as she grounded herself. She wasn't Nora Sinclair tonight; she was Helen O'Donnell, a rising star from a forgotten era. Helen's legacy draped over her shoulders, settling her nerves with an odd sense of calm.

The curtains began their slow ascent, revealing a hauntingly simple set—a grand piano tucked into the corner, a few chosen props hinting at the early 1900s, and a chandelier casting long, wavering shadows over the worn stage floor.

It was perfect. The Majestic Theatre felt alive tonight, like a living entity that was as much a part of the story as she was. Nora stepped into the glow of the stage lights, her body falling into Helen's movements. The hum of nerves still buzzed under her skin, but her voice found its rhythm, her lines slipping from her mouth like they'd always been a part of her.

Across the stage, Alex sat at the piano, fingers poised just above the keys. In that moment, they weren't Alex—they were Zeke Turner, the quiet, intense pianist who had stolen Helen's heart. Nora felt herself drawn to them before they even played a note. Then the music started, soft and melodic, filling the theater with its delicate notes. Her voice followed, weaving through the melody.

Just the two of them were on stage now, exchanging glances as their characters met for the first time.

"You're rushing it!" Nora said as Helen.

Alex—*Zeke* grinned. "Maybe I was waiting to see if you'd catch up."

Something shifted between the characters, pulling the audience into their world. Helen and Zeke's connection grew, their friendship transforming into something deeper, even as the world around them darkened. Nora could feel it as Helen—the pull, the intensity, the unspoken bond forming.

Shadows had a way of creeping in. Catherine, Helen's understudy, slid onto the stage, her every movement sharp and deliberate, her smile thin and cold. She was the embodiment of ambition, her venomous presence. The audience could feel the malice lurking beneath Catherine's every word, a storm waiting to break.

Nora stood center stage, rehearsing Helen's lines, when Catherine's voice sliced through the air like a knife.

"If I were you, Helen, I'd be careful," Catherine said, her tone laced with warning. "There's only so much attention one can draw before people notice."

Helen—no, *Nora*—gave a tight smile, brushing off the veiled threat with practiced ease. But the tension simmered. Catherine's jealousy was festering, twisting into something darker, something dangerous. In a later scene, Catherine appeared alone, clutching a small vial in her trembling hand, her eyes fixed on it with grim intent.

"She doesn't have to die," Catherine whispered to herself, her voice soft. "Just a little something to keep her offstage. Just enough for me to take her place."

The theater seemed to close in around them; the walls pressing in as Catherine's sinister plan took shape in the shadows.

Then came Edward Pritchard.

Nora couldn't see the senator, but she could feel his presence in the audience. His ancestor, Edward, was everything Helen had learned to navigate with care—a charming patron with far too much power and a streak of danger running just beneath the surface. Onstage, Edward's advances toward Helen were polite at first, but with each scene, they grew more insistent, more menacing. Every lingering touch of his hand, every whisper, twisted the tension tighter, making the audience shift in their seats.

"Why fight it, Helen?" Edward growled, his voice a rumble in the intimacy of her dressing room. "I could give you everything you've ever wanted."

Nora—*Helen*—held her ground, her voice steady but cautious. "What I want, you cannot give me," she replied, each word measured. It wasn't just rejection; it was survival. Edward Pritchard's money funded the theater, kept her career alive. But when his patience finally snapped, so did his charm.

In the dim light of Helen's dressing room, Edward's shadow loomed large, his hands closing around her throat. Nora's pulse quickened, a chill running down her spine as Edward's voice rose in fury.

"I've given you everything," Edward hissed, his grip tightening. "And you throw it away for *him*?"

The struggle was swift, but brutal. Helen's hands clawed at Edward's, her breath slipping away. The audience held its breath. The theater plunged into an uneasy silence as the lights dimmed and Helen's body crumpled to the floor. Nora felt it—the finality, the horror. Helen's life had been snuffed out, and with it, something shifted in the air, like the quiet before a storm.

Then came Zeke's trial.

The courtroom scene was stark, the air heavy with injustice. Zeke stood alone, accused of Helen's murder, and Alex—*Zeke's* voice cracked with emotion as they pleaded their case.

"I loved her," Zeke cried, raw grief spilling into every word. "I would never—*I couldn't*. I can prove it."

But no evidence was called for. The gavel came down, sealing Zeke's fate, and in that moment, the world collapsed around him.

Then, something unexpected happened. The actors turned, breaking the fourth wall, facing the audience with solemn expressions. The judge's voice rang out, not to the characters, but to the crowd.

"The court asks you: Who here believes Ezekial Turner is innocent?"

For a long moment, there was silence. Then, one by one, hands rose. A murmur rippled through the crowd, a collective shifting in their seats, and soon, every hand was in the air. It was a moment of redemption, too late for Helen, but not for Zeke. The audience had done what the court had failed to do—they had restored his honor.

As the lights dimmed once more, Alex knelt beside Nora—beside *Helen's*—body, their hand brushing her cheek with a tenderness that made Nora's heart ache. The same soft piano melody from the opening scene played again, but now it was mournful, a lament for what had been lost. The audience was quiet, reverent, as Zeke mourned for Helen in the final, heartbreaking scene.

And then, just as the cast gathered for the curtain call, Nora's eyes flicked to the wings. There they were—Zeke and Helen, hand in hand, watching from the shadows. Nora's breath caught in her throat. No one else seemed to notice, but she saw them as clear as day.

They stood there, smiling, and then they clapped. A small, simple gesture, but it made Nora's heart sing. After everything, they were at peace—together, at last.

As the applause roared around her and the cast took their bows, Zeke and Helen faded into the shadows, their hands still entwined. The stage lights dimmed, the curtain descended. The ghosts were gone. But something had changed. The theater would never feel quite the same again.

When the lights rose again and the curtain lifted for the final bow, the audience erupted into a standing ovation, their cheers filling every corner of the space. Nora blinked, her heart racing, her body still humming with the energy of the night. The cast bowed again, but her eyes found Alex's.

Their gaze met, something unspoken passing between them. Before Nora could second-guess herself, she stepped forward, and Alex moved toward her.

And then they kissed.

Right there, in front of everyone, the applause swelling to a fever pitch. The kiss was unexpected, yes, but it felt right—like the final note of a symphony, perfectly timed and inevitable. It wasn't just an onstage kiss; it was the start of something real. Something that had been building all along.

When they finally broke apart, Nora glanced out at the cheering crowd, her heart full. This wasn't just about Zeke and Helen anymore. This was about second chances, about love that defied time and expectations, about love that found a way through even the darkest of moments.

As Nora looked at Alex, smiling in the glow of the lights, she knew her story was only just beginning.

CHAPTER ELEVEN

Afterword

Thank you for taking the time to read *The Last Act*. While all my stories are special to me, this one holds pieces that are particularly close to my heart, as many elements touch on different aspects of my life. Originally, I included a scene where the senator, moved by the play, decides to dig deeper into Zeke's past, with the hope of securing him a posthumous pardon.

Ultimately, I chose to remove that scene. I wanted my story to focus on love prevailing, hope, and a happy ending—even if it's not the one Nora and Alex originally envisioned. *The Last Act* touches on some darker chapters of our history, and while I never want to overlook those moments, that wasn't the primary aim of this narrative.

In my research, I came across some invaluable resources I'd like to credit, including a podcast episode titled "Illuminating the Unseen" (https://www.oldnorth.com/itu/) and the New England Innocence Project (https://www. newenglandinnocence.org/).

About the Author

B eth Connor is a weaver of tales, captivated by writing and fueled by a love for storytelling.

Beth's creative pursuits are a reflection of her life philosophy, and she is always searching for new ways to expand her knowledge and understanding of the world. She has a keen eye for detail and a remarkable ability to create vivid, dynamic settings that resonate with her audience.

Beth's talent has earned her recognition as the author of several published works, including the novel "Hollow City" The Isdralan Chronicles Series, and the Kindred Spirits Mysteries, as well as a contributor to many anthologies. Beth is also an accomplished audiobook narrator and the host of the popular podcast, "Crossroads Cantina."

Despite her many endeavors, Beth remains down-to-earth and dedicated to living authentically, true to her passions and values. She resides in the Pacific Northwest with her husband, two children, and canine companions, who bring her boundless inspiration and delight.

Also by

ALSO BY BETH CONNOR:

Hollow City

Lake 40

The Isdralan Chronicles:

Micah and the Candles of Time

Prodigy of Flame

Bridge of Blood and Thornes

Kindred Spirit Mysteries:

The Secret of Misthaven Island

Bridging the Heart

The Curse at White Pines